Cover by germancreative @ fiverrr.com

Mirror of Grace

Jane C R Reid

Disclaimer

This is a complete work of fiction. All names, characters, businesses, places, events, historical events and incidents are either the products of the author's imagination or used in a fictional manner.

© Copyright 12/2/19 Jane C R Reid
All Rights Reserved

ISBN: 9781795477994

FOR DAD

"But thy eternal summer shall not fade"

William Shakespeare

Mirror

What is this image that I see?

A spectre of you, or is it me?

Are you a mirage, or is it true?

That you are me, and I am you?

Prologue

'There she is!' the man shouts. Leaving the drawbridge, I steer my horse sharply to the right and work him into a fast run through the long grass. The craggy terrain is hazardous, with menacing rocks hidden beneath the undergrowth, and at times Pharaoh struggles to grip on the boggy ground. Now I know how the deer feels on the hunt, paralysed by fear of impending death. The thud of hooves and men's shouts seem to become ever louder, echoing all about me. I am panicked, my heart beating frantically, hammering in my ears. Adrenalin pumps through my veins like ice and electric shocks shoot through my head. I am the prey chased by a pack of rabid dogs, riding for my life against all the elements as wind and rain lash at me, mud flies and the heavy thud of hooves echo all around. Calling out to Mother Mary, I urge my horse on yet faster, then dare to snatch a look over my shoulder to see how they are advancing, yet all is but a haze….

Chapter 1, Cornwall 1347

'May I have the pleasure my lady?' he asks, audaciously holding his arm aloft. I place my hand atop of his, tentatively looking around to see if others may be watching.

'You may', I respond crossly, 'but really Sir William, you ought adopt more subtlety to deter the wagging of tongues'. I find his demeanour overly bold, and since merriment is scarce here at Farstoan Castle, gossip is rife. He bows his head to one side with a small smile of apology and once again I find myself succumbing to his beguiles, gazing at the ground to avoid being drawn into his dark eyes.

Sir William is roguish and conceited and so unlike my husband Edward, whom ten years my senior, is of a sober disposition, with little interest in social graces. William, skilled in the art of charm, is in the habit of bedazzling the ladies, with his eyes ever a-wandering and a smile that brightens the walls of this cold dank castle. For there are few men here, who are either too young, old or unfit to fight in the war against the French, unless they have pressing assignments here. William has a letter of pardon from his physician proclaiming an affliction of the breathing sickness that impedes his ability to fight. It would seem to me a prudent choice to be here in the company of ladies where husbands are absent, as opposed to a battlefield adorned in blood. He is cousin to our host here, haughty Lady Matilda, whose own husband is away fighting.

I would reckon on Sir William being a gentleman who has ever been pampered and spoiled by women in his nursery. I cannot say I have ever witnessed evidence of his breathing disease and wonder if he perhaps proffered a small bribe to his physician. It certainly would not be the first time this has occurred amongst gentlemen who are reluctant soldiers.

The gardens are immaculately manicured, with floral scents permeating the air, as we amble alongside a large circular bed of roses arrayed in many colours. It is a dank day and with good fortune, there are precious few walkers in the gardens who would delight in tittle-tattle, embellishing my friendship with Sir William. Though I am sure there are those at their windows watching down on us with prying eyes. I dismiss Henriette, my lady in waiting, from walking behind us. Servants are the very worst culprits of gossip.

'Are you sure you are warm enough out here my lady? We wouldn't want you to catch a chill,' William says.

'Sir, though I may resemble an object of fragility, be not deceived by appearances, for unlike other ladies I enjoy the air when it is fresh, for it affords respite from that rotten castle that reeks of stale smoke, cooking and foul men.' As I speak, I sense the presence of someone behind us, and look back over my shoulder to see Matilda de Bray quickly advancing on us.

'So, it would seem my castle offends you Elizabeth,' she says acridly, apparently overhearing us. William turns to her, removes his cap and bows low in over-stated deference, smiling courteously. 'My lady', he says in a tone that suggests, whether authentic or not, that he is charmed to see her.

She affects a countenance of amusement, as though catching two children playing truant. 'Oh, it is charming,' she says, 'to see you both out in this weather, when you could be snugly ensconced before a warm fire. We are having a feast this evening in preparation of the hunt tomorrow, just a small soirée. I wonder Elizabeth, if you may entertain us with some singing?'

Matilda and I have never seen eye to eye, and she knows well how to torment me. 'I am honoured to be asked, but my voice is not pleasing to the ear. Amusement from your jester would be more favourable.'

'Oh come, my dear, you are merely being modest. I am sure you have the voice of a canary; do you not think so William?' She is mocking me, side glancing William as if there is a secret to be shared between them. He smiles in return.

'No, I am afraid I must decline', I say determinedly, pursing my lips.

'Very well then my dear...' Lady Matilda turns impatiently on her heels and marches back to the castle and I am glad to see her go.

'You know, Sir William, I do so miss my home in Suffolk,' I sigh. 'Were it not for the contemptible sweating sickness, I would be there now, most likely riding Pharaoh across our lands. Since I arrived here, I have barely ridden.'

'Well, we have the hunt tomorrow.'

'Nay, sir, I do not enjoy hunts,' I say churlishly, sensing William flinch at the abruptness of my tone. My childhood, though replete with education, was a lonely one, with insufficient interaction to develop my social skills. I am one of three, with two elder brothers. Edgar is six years my senior, the bridge being too wide for close kinship. Then there is Richard, three years my senior, who at the tender age of six, began his training as a page boy, later to be drafted away to London as an esquire. Consequently, much of my child-hood was spent in the nursery quite alone, save the few occasions my cousins came to stay. Now, Richard, married to our host Matilda, is an acclaimed knight and fighting the French with my husband Edward.

My parents, both now deceased, commanded a strict education for me; a curriculum of Latin, Greek, religion, history, household management, etiquette, music, dance and needlecraft. All the litanies I was instructed to learn and recite did so bore me to the point of tears. All this to secure a good betrothal in order to bring prospects to my family, followed by an expectation to propagate my husband's lineage. On the subject of issue, I am ceaselessly reminded by Edward of my failure in my wifely duties. He brands me feckless and unworthy for not producing him an heir. Many physicians have attended to me, trying out a myriad of tricks and potions, but nothing shall cause it to happen, for I am made powerless by divine refusal.

It is barely surprising that I have a predisposition to loftiness, for my life has followed a succession of affronts from both my father and now my husband. Even my mother was apt to keep her children out of her sight closeted away in the nursery.

I turn to Sir William for it appears my terseness has silenced him. 'Pray forgive my mood, sir, for I do so miss my estate. It is most kind of our Lord and Lady de Bray to accommodate me during these tumultuous times and I do not wish to appear ungracious, but I loathe castles and there are few people here that I have a liking for.'

Sir William looks at me kindly. 'I understand my lady and I shall be glad, should you permit me, to escort you on a ride.' A mischievous look clouds his face.

'Sir, you are amused by something?'

'You shall soon discover I am a tad of a jester, my lady, and a fiendish thought just came to mind. What if we were to lose the hunt tomorrow, just for a-while, and ride off on our own? I could say your horse led you astray and I went to retrieve you?'

I tut, shaking my head, 'really sir!' I say brusquely; yet secretly his suggestion causes me a flutter of excitement.

Chapter 2, Suffolk 2016

I sit up in bed sipping my tea, watching James pulling his black tee shirt over his head. 'You woke me up again,' he yawns.

'Oh, I'm sorry. I had that dream again of being chased on horseback.'

'Yes, you shouted *fetch me my horse*, and you kept kicking me!'

'I really don't know why I keep having that dream, though actually it's more of a night-mare. It's the same every time, trying to get away from all these men chasing me. I think it must be my sub-conscious mind trying to come to terms with my accident. It's so damn real, like re-experiencing it over and over.'

My accident occurred seven years ago, when I was out riding my beautiful stallion, Caesar. Even now I don't remember the fall, or what had caused it, but I recall looking down on my body from above, then being drawn into a long tunnel. My mother was there at the other end in a beautiful garden full of wild flowers and I experienced a feeling of peace and love beyond comprehension. I wanted to stay in this tranquil place, but Mum told me that I must go back. Instantaneously I found myself back in my body, feeling heavy and in a considerable amount of pain. I was told that I had encountered some mild damage to my spinal cord and temporarily would be unable to walk, but with intensive physio and hydrotherapy, along with a modicum of patience, it would hopefully improve with time.

It has been a long haul, but my mobility is more or less back to normal now. My right leg still gets stiff, particularly in the mornings, and I've been left with a slight limp. The worst thing is, in lacking the confidence to ride again, yet I am determined to combat this, since riding has always been my main passion.

'Why don't you go to the doctors?' James sounds a little irritated now. I've noticed before how quickly his moods can switch.

'Why, he can't sort out my dreams?'

'Well, if they are because of your accident, maybe you need counselling. At the end of the day Grace, I need my sleep. I'm no good at work if I'm tired all the time.'

'I'm not sure counselling would help,' I say blankly, biting my lip.

I watch as he ruffles his brown wavy hair. He's a gym instructor who knows just how attractive he is; not a stereotype I would normally go for if I am honest, but I can't deny his attentions have been flattering, at a time of personal vulnerability. In the five years I have been married to Lawrence, I have felt my self-esteem diminish and whilst I know that I am physically attractive, I no longer feel it inwardly. We have had our ups and downs and Lawrence is one of those people in life who has everything and yet is innately unstable. He holds the tenet that if he is suffering, he has the right to inflict it on me.

I am alerted from my daydream by the sound of my mobile ringing. 'It's him,' I say flatly. James rolls his eyes and is about to shout out an expletive, but I stop him in his tracks before answering the phone.

'Hi, where are you? It took you a-while to answer,' Lawrence says, sounding disgruntled.

I sigh, 'I'm just getting up, it's only 8.00 here'.

'So, what are you up to today?'

'I'm not sure yet… how are you?'

I glare at James lighting up a cigarette, but he ignores me.

'The lines crackly, I'll call you back,' I say, hanging up.

'Please James, I've asked you to not to smoke in the house. Can't you just wait?' I regret getting out of bed too quickly when a sharp pain runs all the way down my right leg.

James, cigarette in his mouth, waves his arms in the air, a gesture of surrender. 'Alright, alright, I'm off now.' He grabs his gym bag and rushes out the door.

'Men!', I curse under my breath and the phone rings again. It's Lawrence, but I don't answer it as I must quickly get ready for work. I need to find the right time to tell him that I have a part-time job serving in the local baker's shop, as I know he will be disapproving, questioning my motives. He doesn't like me working, articulating that he provides me with everything I need, and that I should be grateful and happy to be a lady of leisure. Yet I am all too aware that the under-lying rationale is his possessiveness.

Lawrence is on a good salary, working away in Riyadh, Saudi Arabia, for six months at a time. We have a wonderful home here and want for absolutely nothing, but unfortunately the thing we desire above all, we can't seem to have; a child. Fertility tests that Lawrence has undergone in Saudi have shown him to be fully functional, so the problem lies with me, most likely attributable to my accident, since my periods have been erratic ever since.

My mobile stops ringing, then immediately starts up again. I'm in a state of flux with no time to answer. I decide I shall phone him back when I'm on my tea break at work; in the meantime drumming up some excuse for not having answered his calls. The ringing finally stops, but then the house phone starts up. My hands begin to shake, feeling his wrath, even though he is thousands of miles away from me. I imagine him here now, raging, just like he did the day before he left the country, when he hit me full in the face with his fist, all because he couldn't find his car keys, laying the blame on me.

I cover my ears as the ringing seems to become and louder and louder, reminding me of a baby that will not stop crying, no matter what.

Chapter 3

Feeling exhilarated after the ride, I can tell by the way he twitches his ears that Pharaoh, my magnificent horse, has revelled in it too. I quickly work to tidy my hair which has become loose, and smooth down my blue gown beneath the riding cloak. My cheeks feel flushed as a young maid's on May Day. William is standing beneath a mighty oak that looks to have been standing for a few hundred years. It has fast become grey over-head and rain begins to fall. Covering my head with my hood, I quickly make my way to the shelter of the tree.

'You move fast on your horse for a lady,' William says smiling.

'Aye, Pharaoh is but a bold destrier. Your own horse struggled to keep up,' I laugh, carefully disguising the conflict I find myself in. I wonder in God's name what conspired me to play along with his ridiculous antics, sneaking away from the hunt? And yet the child in me is invigorated and inspired by such disobedience, for life is overwhelmingly stifling in that gruesome castle with all its dull occupants. It feels so good to break free, if only for a-while. Besides, Sir William fascinates me, and I am privately exalted that he seeks my company above the other ladies.

He smiles at me devilishly, his eyes dark and fascinating. I find myself looking away, fearful of over-familiarity, and unsure of how to conduct myself in this outlandish circumstance. The child in me steps aside for sedate Beth, questioning what I am in fact doing here at all, for such behaviour is hardly befitting of someone of my standing.

The rain now falls in torrents. William, quite the gentleman, is removing his own cloak. 'Please my lady, take this, you must be cold.'

'Nay, sir, I have no need when I have my own, I reply haughtily.

'Yet I insist madam.' He wraps it around me, then lays his arm about my shoulders. I step away quickly, retreating from the shelter of the tree. William laughs, 'come Beth, you are getting wet.'

I am a little piqued at his boldness in calling me Beth, yet before I have a chance to protest, he has me by the arm, leading me back to him under the tree. Then, with no forewarning, he pulls me towards him and kisses me full upon the lips. I am completely aghast, my breath taken away, horrified yet exalted all at once. This is the first time I have ever been kissed upon the mouth, even my husband has never done so. Edward is a man's man, 'women are for the bed and men for the fighting' is what he spouts. He denounces modern gallantry, believing that men of chivalry are boys in petticoats. He abhors too, the growing movement of disgruntled ladies, rising up and calling for more status. For women are tired of being told they are just for bedding and suckling, when in truth, they are afforded great responsibility when their men are away on the battlefields, killing one another with zest.

It is we women who must take charge of the stately affairs. We are charged to keep tabs on lazy farmers and servants, as well as deal with all the daily disputes. We oversee the kitchens, the storehouses and the stables. It is I who was called to dismiss the stable boy for bringing to burden a kitchen servant by laying with her, sending her back to her family with a small pension, then having to replace her. It is my duty to keep a tight purse on wages for many of our provisions have been lost in the perpetual war. I am left with the dross amongst servants whilst the more robust of men are fighting.

My marriage was not the chosen alliance formed during my infancy. My betrothed was meant to be John, who tragically died from ill health at the tender age of eleven. Soon after, it was determined that I would marry his father, Edward, a man fifteen years my senior, who I liked not at all. He had lost his wife to a riding accident and needed an heir to replace John, who had been their only child. When I heard the wretched news, I withdrew into myself, believing my life to be over.

I draw myself away from William, but he brusquely pulls me back to him and kisses me again. Against all good judgment and reason, I become awash with feelings never experienced before and surrender myself for just one more magical moment. It is as though the walls I have built around myself come crashing down, revealing the real me, like cracking open an egg and finding a baby chick inside.

Abruptly I return to my senses, stepping back from him and stamping my foot like a cross palfrey. 'Really sir, did you never learn gallantry in your nursery? I demand that you take me back to the hunt at once.' He smiles at me, apparently amused at my tirade and wonder if this man ever takes *anything seriously. Then he bows to me. 'My lady Elizabeth, you are amongst the fairest and when you permit the ice about you to melt, an inner beauty reveals itself to match your exquisite comeliness.'*

I tut and make my way to my beautiful grey horse.

Chapter 4

It is deathly quiet, save the crackles from the dwindling fire. Candles throw shadows on the rough-hewn stone walls. The room looks lived-in with two chairs in front of the fireplace facing one another, a bed, heavy oak chest and a small writing table and chair. A huge tapestry covers the wall facing the bed.

I tiptoe through the room like a trespasser, then gasp at the sight of a woman, who looks a little like me, sitting bolt upright in the bed. She looks at me directly, then screams out and her servant girl comes running to her side, wearing a long nightgown, with loose brown curls escaping from her nightcap. 'What is it my lady?' she asks. The woman in bed points at me shouting, 'there, look there, who is SHE?'

'Where, my lady, there is no one there, I promise you, you must have been dreaming?' She is looking all around, but evidently can see nothing.

I wake abruptly to the sound of the phone. Stretching out, I quickly try to re-orientate myself. Since I've encountered difficulties sleeping, I've been catnapping in the afternoons on the sofa, but it's not the best idea in the world. My housekeeper, Margot, brings the phone to me, stone-faced as usual. 'It's your husband,' she says. Still drowsy from sleep, I note how Margot appears to bear a resemblance to the servant in the dream I just had.

Lawrence sounds angry. 'Why haven't you been answering your phone? I've been worried about you, what's going on Grace?' I take a deep breath. 'I dropped it in the toilet yesterday,' I laugh nervously, lying through my teeth. 'It's in the airing cupboard drying out.'

'Well, that won't do any bloody good, will it? I'll have to fire some money over to you to get yourself a new one. I can't believe how careless you are Grace, honestly.'

'I know, but it was just an accident, I'm sorry.'

'Are you sure you are being honest with me? You've been acting suspiciously lately. Is there anything you're hiding from me?'

I bite my lip and seize the opportunity. 'Well, actually I have. I have just started a little job, just part-time at the baker's in town. I was just so bored here without you, I needed to do something.'

'Oh really, well I AM surprised. Why are you always so goddamn secretive? Here I am in Riyadh, in the soaring bloody heat, working all hours just so I can support you and give us both a good lifestyle, and you throw these bombshells at me out of the blue. And you wonder why I don't trust you!' he storms hanging up on me.

I jump as the door opens and James comes bouncing in, humming to himself. 'Hey, are you okay?' He asks, throwing his gym bag on the sofa.

'Oh, it's just Lawrence again. I told him about the job. It would've been easier to keep it from him, but he keeps ringing when I'm at work.'

James looks intently into my eyes. 'You've got to ditch him. The man's a control freak. Anyway, it's my job to cheer you up. How do you fancy a curry tonight?'

'Well, Margot is making pasta,' I reply.

'That witch, she still looks at me like I've just crawled out of the woodwork. Are you sure she's not going to say anything to hubby? I'm sure she's acting as his spy.' The first time James stayed over two weeks ago, Margot caught him sneaking out the back door at six o'clock in the morning. I explained to her that James is an old friend and that he will be staying at the house for a-while. Each morning before she arrives, I ruffle up the linen on the spare bed, but she probably knows what is really going on.

'Not if she wants to keep her job. If I'm honest, I don't trust her either. She makes me feel uncomfortable. She does everything here; cooking, cleaning, tidying up after me and she's a true professional. I've tried to befriend her, but she will only speak when spoken to. Lawrence prefers it this way, which is why he chose her, presumably. He advocates that servants should know their place. I've told him his attitude is Victorian and that I would rather do all the chores myself. It's a big house, but what does he expect me to do all day, especially if he doesn't want me to work?'

'I've told you, if he can keep you here in these walls, he can keep tabs on you. And he employs *her* to spy on you when he's not around.'

'I hope you're wrong about that James, but if you're not, we need to be more discreet.'

'Anyway, I'm hungry,' James rubs his lean stomach. 'So, if it's a choice between a Madras or pasta, curry wins I'm afraid.' He looks at me with dark smiling eyes and as always they draw me in. There is something about those eyes, that I just can't place; some kind of a memory like a déjà vu feeling.

Chapter 5

'Lady Matilda, I really must insist that you find me a new chamber.' Her face is aghast.

'My dear, pray sit and calm yourself,' she says, beckoning me to a window seat. 'If your complaint is damp or draught, you should be mindful that castles were not built as pleasure palaces. We may not be able to provide your own home comforts here, yet it is a sanctuary for you in such times of tumult.'

'Forgive me, for I have no desire to dishonour your beneficence and am most grateful for your protection. But I must insist on moving, since there is a phantom in my room.'

Observing my sister-in-law, it is difficult to deduce whether her dark, intense eyes are beautiful or wicked. She stands before me tall and elegant in her red gown of silk and laughs. 'Well, this is the first I have heard of it. Are you sure you were not dreaming? What of this phantom?' she asks in a mocking voice.

'I saw plainly a lady watching me from the foot of my bed, then disappearing into thin air. I was not dreaming, for in truth, I have not slept a full night since I arrived here. I was wondering if your physician may afford me a remedy?'

Matilda is visibly irritated. 'Very well, I shall send you Master Tenwyn and arrange new quarters for you.' She draws up her skirts and hastens from the room. Peering down at the murky moat water below, I find myself sinking deep into contemplation. I am indeed fortunate to be here under my brother's guardianship and have been trying to avoid thinking too much about Hurst-an-Clays grange, our home in Gippeswic, for fear of descending into a state of melancholy. Most of our staff retreated to their homes, many of whom may have already perished. Accounts suggest that far from rescinding; the disease is fast rampaging through the villages and towns throughout Suffolk. There are also fears of plague eventually reaching our shores from the continent, where it is prolific.

I take myself to the chapel to thank Mary and the saints for my good fortune, and appeal to them to watch over the souls of the afflicted. And I pray for our men in battle, fighting upon muddy fields cloaked in blood and corpses. I cannot recall the last time I allowed myself to cry, but heavy tears now saturate my cheeks, falling upon and staining my blue dress. 'Mother Mary,' I whisper, 'why is the world so cruel?'

The piffle twaddle amongst the ladies about how much they are missing their husbands is most irksome.

'Elizabeth dear, your eyes are red. What has befallen you?' Lady Kathryn enquires. She is Matilda's sister, rather plain in comparison, endowed with small eyes and a wide mouth.

'I am grateful for your concern Kathryn, but it is nothing more than a head pain and lack of sleep.' I say without looking up from my tapestry.

Matilda lets out a loud, impatient sigh. 'Bring forth the minstrels,' she commands a manservant. 'The day is too gloomy, we need some cheer.' Another servant tends to the fire. I sink into my own thoughts of Sir William and our antics yesterday beneath the great oak tree. A flutter rushes through my body and conscience incites me to drop my needle. None of this goes unnoticed by Matilda. 'My dear, we were concerned about you yesterday when you disappeared from the hunt, but I understand my cousin took good care of you,' she says slyly, and I feel the eyes of the other ladies upon me.

I continue intently with my needlework. 'Yes, he was most courteous. My horse can be rather wayward at times, especially in foreign lands to which he is unaccustomed.'

'Such a big horse for a petite lady. Would not a palfrey be more suitable? I am sure the marshal would be pleased to accommodate you.'

'That is most kind, but Pharaoh belonged to Edward and he traded it for another since he was too feral for battle. I asked that I may have him, for it would have been fiendish to put out such a robust creature.' It appears Matilda is not convinced, and I can feel judgment heavy in the air, for it is customary for ladies to ride palfreys, not horses of war. In truth, much to Edward's displeasure, I am more accomplished than him at handling Pharaoh. The horse has a will of steel and it is my belief that he acted out deliberate disobedience towards my husband, in his disliking of him.

Master Tenwyn, the physician, holds audience with me in my new chamber, no doubt the smallest Matilda could find just to spite me. Now I am ensconced close to the top of a turret with far too many steps to venture.

'My lady,' he removes his brown velvet cap and bows courteously. He is a lean man with kindly blue eyes, bearing a rustic complexion, a characteristic of the Cornish people. I take an instant liking to him.

'I understand you have not been sleeping well' he says amiably.

'No, I may not rest at all here, sir, for this place is full of demons preventing it.'

'Do you have a history of fatigue my lady?'

'No, I sleep very adequately at my own residence.' I explain to him the reasons for fleeing the family home.

'It is hardly surprising then that you are unable to sleep my lady. I have here a potion you may take as you retire to your bed and I also recommend steady-paced walks in the fresh air each day.' He places the potion on the table. 'Will that be all?'

I nod, and he retreats from my chamber bidding me farewell.

Chapter 6

'Am I keeping you up?' asks Rosa, placing our drinks on the table as I yawn for the umpteenth time. Unusually, the Laughing Pig is not very busy, assumedly because it is only half way through the month.

'I'm sorry, I'm not sleeping very well at the moment.'

'Something on your mind? Is it your husband being pig-headed as usual?' Rosa asks, whilst checking her mobile for messages.

I smile. 'Well, actually this doesn't have anything to do with Lawrence,' I pause, looking into my glass of beer, wondering where to begin. 'When I was in a coma after my accident, I experienced hallucinations that centred around a castle in medieval times. I can't recall a lot of detail, but I remember it was a hostile environment and I felt trapped there. At the time it felt very real, as if my consciousness had shifted from one reality to another. The thing is, I've been dreaming about this place ever since, and recently I've sort of been having visions about it that are keeping me awake.'

'What sort of visions?' Rosa looks very confused.

'It's the same theme as before. I keep seeing this woman in the castle; funnily enough, she looks a bit like me. It happens usually when I close my eyes and I feel like I'm being pulled into this other reality.' I shake my head. 'It's hard to describe.'

Rosa looks nonplussed. 'Are you sure you're not dreaming?'
'Well, I'm still awake and it's more vivid than a dream. It's a bit like watching a silent movie, but not on a flat screen.'
'Can't you just open your eyes?'
'Yes of course, but when I close them again, nine times out of ten it comes back.' I can tell by Rosa's expression, her eyes the colour of coal, that she has absolutely no comprehension of what I have been saying.
'I know it all sounds crazy, but it's absolutely true Rosa. Another thing that's been happening is that sometimes I recognise people that I know, in these visions. Like you Rosa!' She raises her eyebrows. 'You are just like the mistress of the castle.'
Rosa laughs raucously, tossing her straight dark hair over one shoulder. 'Yeah right, pull the other one Grace. I know I can be a prima-donna, but let's face it, you always were one to over-fantasize.'
I am disappointed, though not surprised, that she doesn't believe me since the whole thing must sound ridiculous.
'Look,' says Rosa, 'I think you're allowing everything to get on top of you. Have you thought about going to the doctors'? They might be able to give you something to help you through this difficult time, perhaps even offer a bit of counselling?'
I don't look up from the table. 'Rosa, I am not mad, and I am not imagining things. It's just the way things have been since the accident. A doctor wouldn't understand any of this anymore than I do. Either he'd give me tranquilisers or refer me to a psychiatrist.'
Rosa reaches across the table for my hand. 'Ok, I'm sorry, it's just that we are all concerned about you. I know you are feeling guilty about the affair, but you're so oppressed when

Lawrence is around. You're not even allowed to see your friends, so I think you should let your hair down while you can.' She leans towards me. 'So, come on, tell me all about gorgeous James.'

It is true that Lawrence disapproves of my friends and while the cat's away, I have been playing, meeting up with people I haven't seen for a long time, usually at the Laughing Pig. It is here where I met James at Helen's 30th birthday bash and it was the first time in years I got drunk. James walked me home and slept on the sofa, too concerned to leave me alone, or so he said.

'We're getting on well, although it's a bit tricky trying to dodge Margot all the time. James is convinced she will tell Lawrence. To be honest, I should never have allowed him to stay over like he does, but he shares a house with three students and they're all so inconsiderate, playing their music loud until the early hours and he can never get any sleep there.'

'Well, yes, and I gather he finds your house rather more comfortable,' Rosa says sarcastically.

'Shit Rosa, I'm playing with fire and don't know what came over me that night.' I bite my lip pointing to my empty beer glass. 'You know, Lawrence would even disapprove of me drinking this. It's fine for him to drink as much as he wants, and woe betide me if I say anything. He says it is a man's sport and there is nothing more unattractive than a woman who is drunk.'

'Sounds Victorian to me! I know I've said it before Grace, but the man's a complete control freak and you should get rid. You deserve to enjoy yourself.'

'Maybe Rosa, but you're not married,' I reply a little abruptly. 'Lawrence is complex. He is insecure because he had a bad upbringing. And then, if it hadn't been for the redundancy, he probably wouldn't have become such a heavy drinker.'

'Well, I'm sorry, you can excuse him all you like. As far as I'm concerned, he's always been a tyrant, you just haven't seen it. It's time to wake up and smell the coffee. I know you have a beautiful house, horse, car and luxuries that some women only dream of, but do you really want to live with a bully? It's a high price to pay. Let's face it, if you were happy, you would never have rebelled like you did, because it's not in your nature to be disloyal.' She points her finger at me. 'His abuse has got worse, Grace, admit it for God's sake. He hit you and he will do it again.' She has said her piece and now sulkily picks up her mobile phone to check it again.

I am apt to shove things under the carpet and her words are like a thorn in my side. Even though I know in my heart that she is right, I still seek to defend the situation that she's referring to, partly because I am embarrassed that it caused me to look weak, and partly because it was so hurtful that I don't even want to admit to myself that, in that moment, hate drove him to it.

'But it was the day before he was going to Riyadh and he always gets nervous before a trip,' I say. 'He couldn't find his keys and I'd probably moved them as I'm always tidying up after him. He didn't actually hit me, he pushed me against the door in temper and the lamp fell on my head.'

Rosa waves her hand at me dismissively, clearly disbelieving me. 'You've already told me your story, but I saw your face afterwards. Anyway, I've seen how controlling he is, saying you need to lose weight when you don't. You're not allowed to wear make-up and he criticizes your clothes. He won't let you work or see your friends … the list goes on.' I start nervously chewing on the nail I broke earlier. Rosa looks irritated and slightly bored, looking around the room.

'I value your advice Rosa, but you don't understand Lawrence like I do. He's a complicated man with a lot of insecurities, but he's also very loving. He sacrifices a lot to provide me with a good lifestyle, working away for six months of the year. I really should end it all with James.'

Rosa is rolling her big dark eyes, gazing dismissively around the pub. 'Well, you can throw him my way,' she quips, then looks at me with a serious face. 'Look, I can remember how fun, independent and confident you were before you met Lawrence.'

She has hit a raw nerve and without thinking, I rise, make a fast retreat for the door and run. I hear Rosa calling after me, but just keep running, from what or to where, I don't know. I nearly knock over an old lady as my foot catches her trolley bag. A deafening ambulance alarm jolts my senses and for a moment I feel as though I am in a vision that mirrors my recurring dream of being chased on horseback.

I stop abruptly to catch my breath, supporting myself against the wall, then moments later I find myself sitting in Charmer's café, gazing out the window at nothing. Gathering my senses, I sip my coffee and watch as the heavens open suddenly, sending those without raincoats or umbrellas running for cover, a few retreating here into the café. The diversion has helped, and I ring Rosa to apologise. I can't afford to lose good friends and she's made me realise that I need to pay serious thought to where I am going in my life. She is understanding and invites me to the Laughing Pig this evening. 'Bring James along, it will be good to see if his personality matches his looks,' she says.

'Ok, it's a deal.' I hang up and see Lawrence has sent me a text message, 'missing you baby.' I smile. As usual, I have exaggerated everything, and it is high time I stopped from being a drama queen. All is well, Lawrence loves me, I love him and that is all that matters.

Chapter 7

1347, France

I write to you from a point of exhaustion, whilst you are safe in refuge and indulging in comforts. Doubtless, you and your company are supping our success. Be not misled, for this fight with the French is no courtly dance. The rains have brought in floods, tainted red with blood from the old and young, of fathers and sons. Our supplies are dwindling, and sickness is rampant in the camp. My wounds are made worse by old aches, for my bones are too aged for fighting. For it is with you, where I should be, making a plump healthy heir. As my wife, you must do your duty and not fail me in this, for what is a man without heirs? As soon as I take my leave of this bloody war, we shall persevere in the cause of sustaining the family line, God willing I survive. I pray you be in good health now and upon my return.

Edward

I read it through, then toss it in the fire, watching the flames fiercely devouring it. I live in dread of my husband's return and his rough grappling beneath the sheets. That I am barren has become apparent and Edward's antipathy towards me grows by the day. He has himself told me that in God's eyes I am unworthy of him. My knees have been made sore with praying to Mother Mary and the saints that one day we may be blessed, else he may toss me aside, in favour of a hen who may lay many eggs at his feet.

We are all positioned within the great hall awaiting Lady Matilda's announcement. She signals her usher to silence the minstrels and a hushed air of anticipation fills the room. She has made a special effort tonight, apparelled in her finest gown of purple, trimmed with fur, and donning the new style tall head-dress, brought over from France. Ever aware of her regal beauty, she cossets the admiring looks from the sparse male company we have here.

'Word has arrived,' she begins, 'that our men are victorious again. They have defeated the French at La Roche Derrien.' We all cheer, some stamping the trestle tables with their fists. Matilda raises her cup, 'therefore tonight we celebrate, but first, let us drink to our men.' We all stand and raise our cups and repeat the chant, 'our men and victory.' I think of Edward's letter and his terse account of the wretched conditions befalling them, victorious or not.

Right on cue, the minstrels start up a cheery jibe encouraging us all to make our way to the dancing area, allowing the servants to clear the tables. The castle always looks its best at night-time, with copious candles beaming shadows on the thick stone walls and the fires seem to take on new life, dancing with more veracity. I look for William and notice him in conference with Lady Elowen, only recently out of mourning for her husband, who died at the siege of Calais. William looks particularly handsome tonight in a dark blue wool doublet and cap to match. He catches my eye, smiling and I avert my gaze.

'It is good news is it not how the war goes in our favour?' says Lady Kathryn, approaching me with her tiny pet mutt in her arms.

'Indeed, though it would be naive to suppose that honey paves the way, that there are heroes and villains as in the tales of children. War is an ugly affliction causing nought but pain and strife,' I say.

'Oh, but our men relish it. For what else would they do were they not kept occupied in this way? Their swords would go rusty and you know as well as I about the upsurge of brawls in times of peace, though I am most impatient for it to end, to have my betrothed return, that we may marry at last.'

I pity Kathryn for her infatuation, for word has it that Henry, her betrothed, is far from the gentleman she perceives him to be. Unbeknown to her, he has eyes for another and has broadcast his intention to annul his alliance with Kathryn.

'May I have the pleasure?' William approaches with his usual charm and aplomb, sending a flutter to my stomach. Kathryn's mutt suddenly leaps from her arms, clearly taking a dislike to him, causing great amusement to us all. I place my hand on William's arm, carefully concealing the fervour I feel as he leads me to the dance area. Our eyes meet as we stand facing one another in readiness of the Estampie dance. I feel an intensity from him, an energy that seems to envelop just the two of us, as we step and twirl to the merry tune. I experience an inner jubilance and joy like never before, wanting the music to ensue forever. When it ends, without wishing to draw further attention, I walk away from him and he follows. 'Why do you always run from me?' he asks. 'Do you think I carry the plague?'

With so many people in the room we find ourselves being pushed close to the fire and I begin to feel faint from the heat. 'I need air sir,' I say, grabbing my skirts and retreating from the room hurriedly. William follows me out into the courtyard. The freshness of the night air quickly restores me.

'How do you fare now Beth?'

'Much improved, thank you, sir. The heat just overcame me.'

'Oh come, Beth, no more formalities, pray call me William.' He stands to face me and looks into my eyes. 'When shall you finally loosen your kirtle?' You know, you truly are the fairest lady of the court.'

'You flatter me, sir.'

He asks for my hand and escorts me to a quiet area around the side of the castle to a small bench, away from prying eyes. Taking my hand in his, he says, 'Beth, be not cold with me, for I have been quite unable to think of anything but you since our embrace.'

'Pray, sir, it was but a foolish indiscretion. Do not take me for a cheap-side hussy,' I look away from him.

He changes tact. 'I know of your husband and his un-couth demeanour.' I look down at my hands clenched in my lap, recoiling from the sudden memory of Edward striking me across the face the day before he left for France. His letter was a harsh reminder of the resentment he feels towards me and I know not when he will be coming back, for he ever prefers to surprise me. His letter suggests that there may be little respite upon his return, since this is his last dance with war.

I am usually accomplished at disguising my pain, yet William has shifted something within me with his *attentiveness and I am quite unable to stifle the moistness from forming in my eyes.*

He draws me to him, and I begin to weep shamefully. 'Beth, dear Beth, I know not your story, but you deserve better. Allow me to proffer you a little comfort.' He strokes my cheek and before I know it, we are kissing with a reckless abandon, and I have no care in the world but to surrender to this man.

Chapter 8

There seems to be some kind of banquet going on. The lady I usually see is there dressed in a sky blue gown, in conversation with a woman carrying a tiny dog in her arms, which to everyone's amusement jumps to the floor when a man approaches them. He escorts the lady in blue away and they join a party of people to dance. Then they go outside and walk for a-while before sitting on a bench. The man comforts her as she cries. It would appear they are courting, but in a clandestine manner, so perhaps one or both of them are married.

I am startled awake by James, shouting 'boo' in my ear. I groan and stretch, propping myself up on the sofa. 'No wonder you can't sleep at night if you're cat-napping all the time,' he says.

'I know, it's a bad habit,' I yawn, struggling to bring myself back to the present. I leap up when I notice the time on the clock.

James and I walk in the pub together and I notice Rosa and our circle of friends sitting at a round table by the glowing fire. It's unusual to have the fire lit so early, but it has been unusually cold for this time of year. Rosa is, as always, the centre of attention, wildly gesticulating and laughing. I have known her since secondary school and at thirty-two years old, she still enjoys the single life. She is no advocate of monogamy, preferring casual relationships, 'mates with benefits' as she puts it. If her lovers become possessive or get too close, she ditches them without a second thought, swiftly moving onto the next one.

As we make our way to the table my phone starts to ring. 'You get the drinks in,' I say to James, rushing off to the ladies to answer the call.

'It's taken you a long time to answer. I thought you'd broken or lost your phone again. Where are you?' It's Lawrence.

Aware of the background noises, he will know I am not at home. 'I've had to pop out for some milk,' I say feebly.

'I've told you before, you need to use Margot for errands like that. God knows I'm paying her enough.'

'I know, but I don't like taking advantage. How's your day been?'

'Bloody awful, busy, hot and sweaty. The air-con broke down. I hate it here Grace. If it weren't for the fact they pay me a bloody fortune, I'd tell them to shove the job. I've been doing some thinking. I want us to go to the doctors when I get back, to get to the bottom of why you won't get pregnant. I'm thinking we should try for IVF.'

I bite my lip nervously. For two long years I would be gutted each time my period started and dreaded telling Lawrence, seeing the disappointment on his face and feeling his simmering anger. But since he has been away, I've been wondering how a baby would affect our relationship. Would it bring us closer or widen the gap between us even further? The distance between us has afforded me the opportunity to look deeper into our relationship and I now see how Lawrence's Jekyll and Hyde tendencies have, over time, served to deplete my power and I have to admit I have become a shadow of myself.

'Ok, I'll look into it, do some research,' I say, eager to end the conversation and get back to my friends. 'Anyway, I'd better go as I'm at the shop now.'

'Oh, thanks! Here I am, three thousand bloody miles away, working my nuts off in this freaking heat, missing my wife, and you can't wait to get rid of me for a pint of bloody milk. Thanks a lot!' he rages hanging up on me. I notice my hands are shaking. I know that he will sulk forever now, so I try ringing him back, but he's refusing to answer.

When I arrive at the table, James is sitting next to Rosa chatting animatedly and I notice she is blatantly flirting with him, adjusting her hair and using her eyes seductively. I have seen it so many times before. I am a little jealous, even though I know she would never betray me as a friend.

'Did you get the drinks?' I ask James.

'No, it's all my fault, I've been collaring him,' says Rosa smiling mischievously as he makes his way to the busy bar. She winks at me, 'um, not bad. You've done well there Grace, not just good looking either,' she says, summing up her appraisal of him. Before I can answer her, my mobile rings again. Rosa can tell who it is by my facial expression and rolls her eyes. 'Just don't answer it', she says crossly, but I am already making my way back to the toilets.

Ten minutes later I return downhearted after listening to Lawrence's onslaught. James is busy in conversation with Rosa and Claire. By now all the seats have been taken. The pub is heaving, and I find myself wedged close to the fire. I suddenly begin to feel faint, so make my way outside to the beer garden to get some air. It is attractively lit with coloured fairy lights dotted all along the hedges. I shiver a little in the cold night air and take in a long deep breath.

'Hey Gracie,' one of Rosa's friends Tanya approaches me. 'Let me introduce my cousin, Mason, he has recently moved here from Cornwall. The fresh air I came out for, becomes at once contaminated by the smoke from their cigarettes. I shake Mason's hand, aware at once of his calm demeanour and take an instant liking to him.

'Have we met before?' he asks quizzically?'

'I don't think so,' I reply, but when I study him more closely, there does seem to be something familiar about him, his eyes in particular. As I look at him, my vision blurs over and his face changes right before my eyes. For a split second I recognise him from my visions as the man who I took to be a doctor, that I recall handing the lady in blue a small bottle, like some sort of a potion. He had the same eyes and expression as Mason but, unlike him, he donned a meticulously trimmed beard. The vision is only brief but sharp and clear, causing a certain amount of disorientation as I begin to lose my bearings. 'Are you alright?' Mason reaches his arm out to support me, then leads me to a picnic bench and places his jacket around my shoulders.

Just then, I notice James walking towards us and Mason retreats. James sits next to me drawing his arm around my shoulder. 'Are you ok baby, what are you doing out here?'

I tell him that I was feeling faint. I have tried before to explain my visions to him, but like most people he is scared of what he doesn't understand, so dismisses them out of hand. He looks over at Mason and I sense a tinge of jealousy. Then he removes the jacket from my shoulders, replacing it with his own and draws me towards him and kisses me, more I believe as a signal to Mason, than from genuine passion. Guilt has followed me around like a shadow ever since I met James. Perhaps Rosa is right, that I do deserve a little happiness. James makes me feel so good, reminding me of what love should be about. It has only been a few weeks, barely long enough to know if the connection is one of lust alone, and James is renowned for being a ladies' man. At 33, I am five years older than him, whereas Lawrence is ten years my senior. I think back to when I first met him five years ago and how loving he was then. In hindsight, I wish he had not managed to persuade me to marry so quickly, when we didn't really know each other, but I now believe that his main motivation was driven by his desire to have a child. As soon as the honeymoon ended everything changed, his interest in me waning overnight. All those small nuances of mine that used to amuse him, all of a sudden seemed to become huge annoyances.

As we kiss, I hear a pinged message on my phone. I know it will be from Lawrence.

I read it later when I am next alone.

'Sorry baby, you know what I'm like. Please try harder not to make me so angry. x'.

Chapter 9

Master Tenwyn enters my chamber, removing his dripping cap and shaking it. Evidently, he has been caught up in the storm.

'Pray be seated here by the fire Master Tenwyn, your clothes are soaked through.' Henriette, fetch us some ale.' He hands her his cloak and sits in the chair opposite me.

'Thank you, the storm has subsided since I am now within the castle walls,' he laughs. 'How may I be of service today?'

'I am finding the potion you gave me for sleep too potent, for it is causing me to see things.'

'Can you be more specific my lady?'

'Well, to begin with, it makes me very fatigued, but when I close my eyes, oftentimes I see people in strange attire and odd happenings, barring me from sleeping until much later.'

Master Tenwyn is quietly studying me. 'Indeed, it is a strong potion, perhaps not suitable for you. Would you describe your visions as dream-like?'

'Yes... No; it is difficult to say. They appear to be real, which sounds ridiculous I know. I experience them even though I am not actually asleep, if that makes sense.'

Master Tenwyn notices Henriette is listening in on us and he addresses her sternly. 'I would that you allow us to speak in private.' She scuttles away like a sulky kitten.

'I apologise my lady, but it pays to be circumspect with servants, for however diligent they may be in their work, they are apt to cause mischief in the taverns with their loose tongues. The Cornish are more superstitious than folk from other parts and discussions of an esoteric nature all too often ignites gossip.'

'But pray, sir, it is a more suitable potion that I require. I do not understand your talk of the esoteric.'

Master Tenwyn shifts in his chair. 'My potions are strong and pure, prepared by my good lady wife. They are based on knowledge brought to us by many generations in my family. Some of the plants that we use for healing, may at times trigger an unveiling of realms beyond the veil.'

'Pardon me, sir, but why would anyone wish to see these hidden realms?'

Tenwyn shrugs his shoulders. 'There are many of my kind here in Cornwall who have the gift of seeing and then there are those who choose to use the plants to help improve their inner sight.'

'And you, sir, are you able to do this?'

'Pray, my lady, hold your voice a little softer, since there are those who do not understand, who would accuse unfairly.'

'You speak of witchcraft,' I whisper.

'That is a term given by those who are in fear of what they do not understand. Those more knowledgeable describe it as a gift.'

This is all most perplexing, and I pause for a moment to reflect before responding. 'Well, I know not much of what you speak, but I trust you. Pray, tell me what my visions have to do in all of this.'

Sir William looks at me kindly. 'It is too early to tell as yet. Are you fearful, or would you seek to investigate them a little further?'

I hesitate. 'No, I have no fear. In truth, they are somewhat interesting, but may probing do any harm?'

'As long as there is no fear, I cannot see why, my lady. If the potion becomes too much for you, I suggest you cease using it, or at least take a little less. Perhaps we may re-evaluate it all in a week or two?'

'Very well Master Tenwyn, I bid you thanks and farewell,' I say rising from my chair.

Chapter 10

'Come on Grace, I've finished my lunch and you've barely touched yours.' Rosa looks at her watch impatiently. 'I have to get back to the office soon.'

'I'm not hungry,' I say pushing the plate away. Rosa rolls her eyes, and we are interrupted by Eva, the bar maid, trailed by Alfie, her tiny Cockapoo, who is always at her feet. 'Tom has proposed to me, look,' she says excitedly, flashing a bedazzling sapphire and diamond ring at us.

'Great,' says Rosa, 'so when's the happy day going to be?'

'Well, we haven't set a date. Tom's not in any hurry, but it's such a great feeling being engaged.' I'm happy for Eva but Tom has a reputation for being a ladies' man and I personally wouldn't trust him. There have been times since my accident when I have experienced powerful insights and in this moment I have the feeling that there will be no wedding, that Tom will betray her. As I watch her speak animatedly, I realise she resembles the lady in my recent vision, whose tiny dog jumped out of her arms when a man approached. I look at Eva's own dog nestled up against her ankles, always there at her side.

Eva rushes back to the bar to serve an agitated customer and Rosa startles me back to reality. 'So, come on, what's up Grace, is it your arsehole of a husband again?'

'Oh, I don't know Rosa, everything's getting on top of me at the moment; Lawrence, lack of sleep and there's the dilemma with James.'

'Well, I've told you what I think. You need to run a mile from that husband of yours and start to live again.'

I laugh nervously, 'it's not as simple as that.'

'James is a great catch and it's good to see you out again. Grace you've forgotten how attractive you are. I'm glad to see you're putting on a bit of weight and are growing your hair again. Lawrence wants you thin and dowdy, unattractive to men, camouflaging you from your beautiful self.'

'These days Lawrence can't pay me a compliment without following it up with an insult. He would say, *that dress is nice, but make sure you hold your tummy in.* He always makes me feel like I'm short of the mark.'

'Yeah, it's a classic tactic for someone who feels insecure about themselves, to put the other person down. He is terrified of losing you. The problem is it usually backfires in the end. Have you told James about your visions?'

'Well I've tried, but he just thinks I'm bonkers too. He's there as well; in my visions I mean.'

'Well, whatever. I'm sorry love, I'm out of my depth here, but I can't help but think that Lawrence is putting you under a lot of stress, even in his absence, and that might be causing...'

'No Rosa,' I say loudly, drawing strange looks from the couple at the next table. I lean towards her and whisper, 'I am not mad.'

'I'm not saying that Grace. Maybe you are psychic?'

'Whatever that means ...'

Rosa rolls her eyes. 'Have you decided if you're going to carry on with him?'

'I don't know, I change my mind about it every day. I tell myself it's wrong, then Lawrence pisses me off again and I justify carrying on for a bit longer.'

'Well, you need to make up your mind. Anyway, changing the subject, James has agreed to coach me in tennis skills. I'm next to useless, can't do backhanders to save my life.' She rises to her feet. 'Must dash, Mike won't be happy if I'm late making his coffee. He's such a chauvinist but I guess as his PA it's my job to keep him sweet. Shouldn't you be at work today?'

'I've quit, I just can't face the hassle at the moment.'

'Oh, don't tell me, Lawrence again.' She points her finger at me saying, 'stop giving your power away,' as she rushes off.

I finish my lager and watch the passers-by through the old leaded window. I become aware of my vision blurring over and the town scene changes, reverting back several hundred years, from concrete roads to cobbled streets, cars to carts and from modern to medieval people. As always, the apparition lasts only for a moment before reverting back.

When I arrive back home, Margot is sitting at the kitchen table eating her sandwiches and reading a newspaper. However discreet she is, I always find her presence intrusive. James is coming over tonight and I have promised to cook a special meal, so I instruct her to take the rest of the day off. Anyone else would be pleased to be stood down, Margot leaves with apparent reluctance.

My phone rings just as I am about to climb in the shower. I curse, expecting it to be Lawrence, but it is from an unknown number. 'Hi, it's Mason, do you remember we met the other night?'

'Oh hi, Mason, yes I do. You loaned me your jacket.'

'Right. Look, I bumped into Rosa just now and she mentioned that you're having a bit of a weird time with visions and things.'

'Err yes, very weird.'

'Well, I just wondered if you'd like a listening ear? I'm not claiming to be an expert, but I do know a little about psychic phenomena and stuff.'

'Well,' I find myself hesitating, not sure if this is the route I want to go down. 'It's kind of you Mason, but I'm not really into that sort of thing and I don't think additional weirdness would be helpful.'

'Hey, there's no need to be frightened. I'm not a black magician or anything I just think I may be able to offer a little support and perhaps a fresh perspective on things, that's all.'

'Oh, well ok then, thanks Mason. Just being able to talk to someone who doesn't accuse me of being mental would be helpful,' I laugh.

We make the arrangements for me to visit him tomorrow and then I start to prepare myself for the evening. All is ready downstairs and the food is cooking slowly, perfectly timed for James' return. When I get out of the shower my phone pings. It is a message from James:- *Will be late, an hour or so, sorry I forgot, have a tennis lesson booked after work x.*

All that rushing, the cleaning, prepping; all for nothing. The meal will be ruined. Great! Obviously coaching Rosa is more important than a dinner date with your girlfriend. Instead of blow-drying my hair, I wrap it in a towel, leaving my lovely new blue dress on the bed. I wrap myself in my dressing gown and go downstairs and pour myself a large glass of the expensive red wine I had bought especially for the meal. The steaks stay in the fridge and the vegetables go in the bin, for I have no appetite to eat anything, not now and I certainly have no intention of feeding James.

Chapter 11

I reflect upon the strange apparition I had last night after taking Tenwyn's potion. I saw a woman on a sizable horse, like Pharaoh, riding hastily through the countryside. She donned a strange shaped head-dress, with her hair hanging down her back in a long untidy binding. Her attire was odd, like that of a man, yet she wore no cloak. Without warning, her horse tripped and went down. The impact brought me straight back to my senses and I know not what happened next. I have no idea what to make of these images that Tenwyn defines as 'viewing beyond the veil.' I think I must be going quite mad.

William and I are being as prudent as possible, though I am certain that tongues are wagging since we spend a lot of time together. Our alibi is in his schooling of me to better manage Pharaoh, being such a bulk of a horse with unruly tendencies, though in truth he responds better to me than he would William or any other man. Each day we ride out to our sanctuary in the depths of the forest where we share precious moments of intimacy. It is assuredly the happiest time of my life, feeling able to withdraw my guard for the first time ever, surrendering to passion and loving attentiveness. I afford myself this brief sojourn of joy whilst I am able, for when my husband returns, he shall resume his fiendish ways and iron fist governing.

I adjust my gown and remove my head-dress, allowing my hair to cascade freely over my shoulders, the way William likes it. We are in a secluded spot, but I still check anxiously that we are quite alone before joining William on the blanket he has spread upon the ground. He frames my face in his hands, looking into my eyes and we kiss. Then his hands begin to wander, and I stop him. He looks at me in surprise.

'Pray sir, you are most impatient,' I retort. 'It occurs to me that I know so little of you, for it is hard getting to know one another in the castle, with prying eyes at every corner. May we not talk for a short while?'

William is irked and begins to fidget. 'What do you want to know?' he asks gruffly.

'Well, what of your wife?'

'Ah Mary, she is not of sturdy health, steeped in melancholy of her mother's death. I do not believe she wishes to be well again. She is quite a hopeless cause.'

'Really, you have given up on her sir? Should you not be at her side a little more?'

'It is not I, but she who has given up and verily I am glad to be here, away from her cheerless presence.'

'Do you have heirs or beneficiaries?'

'Two daughters, both quite as dour as their mother.'

'And just what is your role here at Farstaan?'

'Why, I am here to watch over my cousin in her husband's absence, along with her guests such as you and the other ladies.'

'Methinks Matilda is more than capable of looking after herself. Though it is a most dull place with so many women and few men. I have seen how you revel in the admiration of the ladies vying for your attention.'

'Ah, but it is your admiration only that I seek.'

'And were it not for your ill health, would you prefer to be there with the men in France?'

He laughs loudly. 'Well, indeed I should prefer to be nursing my wounds on a marshy battlefield of corpses than surrounded by beautiful ladies!'

'Yet most of the men relish it, they are raised to it and love to fight.'

'I, madam, are not most men. I am no fool.'

We both hear the sound of an advancing horse and jump to our feet simultaneously. I run quickly to Pharaoh, in the pretence of attending to him, whilst William hurriedly folds away the blanket. It is a squire messenger who approaches him and after sharing a few words, hands him a sack-cloth bundle before turning on his horse and departing.

'Why did he give you that?' I ask.

'He has more despatches to make, so I offered to deliver them to Matilda.'

Later that afternoon I learn that the package included a letter for me. I feel anxious as I break Edward's seal, since he only writes to me when he has words of chastisement to proffer. Henriette stands watching me, waiting for me to break the seal. She is apt to be meddlesome, just as Master Tenwyn cautioned, and I trust him as he has a sense of knowing what others may not. I shall speak to Edward of replacing her when he returns. 'Leave me,' I demand, and she sullenly turns and walks away.

1347, France

I understand from my brother's correspondence from his wife, that you are unable to control that brutish beast of a horse. I regret indulging your absurd sensibilities of saving it from the slaughter, where it should have been destroyed long ago.

You shall madam accept a palfrey from my brother's stables befitting a lady of your standing and rid yourself of the beast. Be done with your ridiculous fancies.

Edward

I perceive the rancour in his words, for I have embarrassed him before his family. This is the work of my conniving sister-in law, Matilda. She has seen through our plan and is doing her best to thwart it. 'I loathe her,' I shout out, 'and I abhor this place.' I throw a pewter goblet to the wall, good wine spilling and forming a red puddle on the floor like blood. Henriette appears from the shadows making me jump. 'Clear it at once!' I command.

Chapter 12

'I've found a potential buyer for the horse Grace. I don't see any point in keeping it if you can't ride it anymore.'

I am in shock. 'No Lawrence, you can't do that. Caesar is my horse and not yours to give away.' I say defiantly.

'You're being selfish. It's not fair keeping a horse that can't be exercised. He's costing me a fortune for nothing. Besides, he could've killed you, he's too big. Let's face it, it's doubtful you'll ever ride again, but if you do, I'll get you a pony.'

'No Lawrence, I don't want a pony, I want Caesar. I just need to get a bit more strength back in my legs and then I'll be able to ride again. My physio is confident and so am I. In the mean-time, I was thinking of contacting Kelston riding club to see if they can use him for their classes.' What I haven't told Lawrence is that it is not just the lack of strength in my legs holding me back, for I have also lost my nerve. The thought of rever riding again cripples me and I am determined one day to overcome this mental block.

Lawrence pauses for breath, never one to be beaten. 'Well, I think you're being ridiculous and unrealistic. Even if you were ever to ride again, if you had another fall, you'd probably kill yourself the next time.' Caesar is my pride and joy and has been with me for much longer than Lawrence has. He will not take him off me, on this I am resolute, even if I have to go back to work to pay for his upkeep myself.

'It won't happen, but if it did, then the responsibility is all mine.'

'What is it with you Grace? Why are you so bloody minded these days? Why can't you accept when you are wrong?' and he hangs up.

I am still reeling from our conversation when James saunters in, nonchalantly throwing his gym bag and keys on the sofa. I haven't yet forgiven him for being late last night after all the effort I'd gone to. 'Still sulking?' he asks casually, searching for the television remote. I really can't face another confrontation right now.

'Look James, I just think you were insensitive when I'd gone to all that effort to cook you a special meal. You didn't even give me notice.'

He walks towards me holding out his long arms, his dark eyes radiating charm. 'Will you forgive me?' he asks in a soppy voice. Before I can answer, my vision begins to cloud over, and I know what is happening but am powerless to stop it. James' face morphs into an image of another man, who I recognise as the clandestine lover of the lady in blue. If it weren't for the beard, he would be a dead ringer for James. As always, the apparition disorientates me, even though it only lasts a brief moment. I reach down, grasping hold of the arm on the sofa, and ease myself into it. 'Are you ok?' James asks.

I quickly regain control, 'yes fine,' I say noticing the clock, suddenly remembering I have arranged to meet up with Mason.

'Hey, where are you going?' James asks as I grab my coat and keys.

'Won't be long, just catching up with a friend. There's a quiche in the fridge that Margot prepared, or we can have a takeaway later.' I rush out the door before he has the chance to ask any more questions.

Mason hands me a mug of coffee, then sinks into a huge bean bag next to the fireplace. 'You'll have to excuse the mess, but I only moved in two weeks ago,' he says casually. There are a few unopened boxes in the corner of the small room. 'I want to give it a lick of paint when I get around to it, but at the moment I have to give priority to the new job.'
'Where are you working?' I ask.
'As a support worker at the Tobias special needs school. That's the reason I moved up here.'
'Were you sad to leave Cornwall? It's such a lovely place. I used to go there a lot as a child on holiday.'
'Not really, you're right it is a great place, though it's become far too touristy for my liking.'
I am interrupted by my mobile, it's James. 'Hi, look I can't talk now, will catch you later, ok?' and I hang up watching Mason lighting an incense stick and tea-light candles on the mantlepiece.
He has a quiet calm manner and I feel completely at ease in his company, finding myself opening up to him, telling him about all the weird things that have been happening to me since the accident. I end by asking him, 'so do you think I am mad like Rosa does? Do you think I should see a doctor?'
Mason looks thoughtful and deep in reflection. 'I come from a different perspective on these sorts of things. It's not uncommon for people who experience a significant trauma or NDE, which is a near death experience, to open up psychically.'

I fidget uncomfortably. 'Sorry Mason, but you've lost me there.' My phone rings again. This time it is Lawrence. I stop the call and will have to pay for it later, no doubt. 'I'm so sorry Mason, I'm turning the damn thing off.'

He smiles and continues. 'Ok, so our psychic centre is our true knowing. Attitudes around psychic phenomena change throughout time. The pagans worshipped nature, the Victorians were big on séances, then in my mum's era it became popular to read tea leaves and crystal balls. Now, channelling, remote viewing, past life therapy, crystal work and healing are all popular modules and more and more people are waking up to their own innate abilities, rather than relying on so-called gifted people, because we are all capable if we are open to such concepts.'

'Are you able to do any of these things?' I ask.

'My grandmother and mother both have mediumistic abilities and I used to see spirits as a child. Most people are actually born psychic, but it is drummed out of them as they grow older. In my case, my mum encouraged it.'

'And your father?'

'Well, I've not seen him since I was four years old, but according to Mum, he didn't buy into it.'

'So, are you saying this is what has happened to me, that the accident caused me to become psychic?'

'It does sound like it, but remember, psychic phenomena are a whole host of things. In your case I wonder if you might be tapping into a parallel lifetime, that appears to be overlapping with this one. A lot of people have the means to explore their past lives, including myself, usually under hypnosis or by using meditation. But you seem to have the capability of spontaneous recall without the props. Of course, concepts such as these are not recognised, as reincarnation does not fit into our societal religious systems. Cultures in other parts of the world however, particularly in the eastern hemisphere, acknowledge reincarnation as fact, believing that we experience lives in different roles over and over as a means of learning and evolving. To us, lifetimes appear linearly to help us gain a perspective, but like Einstein said, time is an illusion, and, in essence, all of our lives are happening simultaneously, which is nigh on impossible for us humans to integrate. The only way we can make sense of everything is in applying continuum; left signifying the past, right the future and placing all in order of sequence.'

I sigh. 'Wow, there's a lot to take in, but it's a relief to be talking to someone who doesn't think I'm completely mad. What I find so difficult is that the two realities sometimes seem to be intertwined and I find it hard enough dealing with this life, let alone another as well.'

I daresay confusion is written all over my face, but James looks at me patiently with his kind pale blue eyes. 'I'm sorry, this is such a hard thing to grasp, but as they say, truth is stranger than fiction. It's a sad fact that many people have been persecuted over the ages due to a lack of understanding, burned as witches or locked away in mental asylums. In modern times, suppressant drugs are issued to people who complain of time distortion. There are also hallucinogenics capable of inducing these types of experiences.'

All this information is baffling, and I wonder if it's true that we come back again and again. Why ever would we want to do that? 'So, ok, if it's true that we experience all our lifetimes simultaneously, why is it I singled out this one over another?'

'I would say that your accident jolted something that relates you specifically to that lifetime. There is perhaps some karma or unfinished business to work through.' Mason leans forward clasping his hands. 'Look, I'm sorry for bombarding you with all this and I know how hard it is to take in, as it's all new to you. My philosophy is that knowledge is power. If you know what's going on, it's easier to deal with. It's up to you Grace, you can walk out that door saying this is all a load of bollocks, or you can allow me to help you through it all. I can't promise anything, but at least I am prepared to listen.'

'Well, thanks Mason. I will have to go and try to digest it all,' I laugh. 'Whether you are right or wrong, you are the only person who will listen to me. Please, yes, I need your support.'

'Fine, check in with me next week and we'll have another chat. I would suggest you start paying more attention to the visions and perhaps documenting them.'

I walk out of Mason's flat feeling a little strange, yet at the same time hugely relieved.

Chapter 13

'If you receive any instructions to take away my horse, I forbid you to do it. The horse belongs to me and is mine to do with as I shall.' The marshal looks bemused at my outpouring and shakes his head.

'Who my lady would be commanding this? With due respect, I can only take orders from my mistress.'

'Do not be concerned with your mistress,' I say crossly, 'for it is no affair of hers.' I turn, unwittingly stepping in a clod of mud, splattering my clean gown and silently berate myself for my rashness in not having exchanged my delicate shoes for boots.

Next, I hasten to the solar, where Matilda is seated with her usual entourage of ladies, all dutifully performing their stitchery. She rises to her feet in surprise at my boisterous entrance. Her height makes her an imposing character. 'Why Elizabeth, what troubles you?' she asks in a voice of false virtuousness.

'This, Matilda; THIS!' I present her with Edward's letter and watch as she reads it slowly, showing no expression upon her face.' A hush fills the room, the ladies having stopped their jabbering to eavesdrop, furtively passing eye contact amongst themselves.

'Well, my dear, I cannot say I am surprised at this. Why would my brother-in-law not be concerned for his wife's welfare and safety? It is most unnatural for a lady to ride such a beast. Have I not offered you one of our obedient palfreys? Your husband my dear is right, the horse is neither fitting nor safe for you.'

'Spare me your meddling Matilda,' I say loudly, aware of the ladies gasping under their delicate breaths. 'Pharaoh belongs to me and no one has the right to take him away. Plainly it is beyond your comprehension that I may favour the challenge of his rough ride over a palfrey's gentle steps. The charge through the countryside thrills me, proffering me freedom from these stifling walls.'

Matilda is stone faced. 'Even if your husband forbids such senseless recklessness?'

'I shall deal with my husband upon his return since it is MY issue madam.' I turn on my heels and bolt from the solar. I know I have alienated myself even more with the company here but have no care. My rides with Pharaoh are the only thing that keeps me sober in this hostile castle with filthy guards and gossip-mongering ladies for company. I cannot be like them, sitting all day working with tapestry and fixing chemises. Such would assuredly drive me to distraction.

On returning to my chamber Henriette informs me that Sir William called by enquiring if I desired to ride out with him today. I must chastise him for his indiscretion, coming to my chamber so, for such an action would surely incite gossip and I may not trust my maid. Right now, I would slap the smugness from her face.

'Fetch my riding clothes,' I command, 'my warmest ones.'

Despite the weather being damp and chilly today, I am exhilarated to be free from the confines of the castle on my magnificent horse with beloved William. I still know not if his charm holds any depth, yet he is my only true friend here.

We find our usual spot and he sets the blanket upon the ground and arranges our picnic. Then he reaches over to kiss me. 'Sir, pray wait until at least we have eaten,' I laugh. I tell him about the letter, and he chuckles at my ire and obstinacy. 'Why do you think he instructed this?' he asks.

'It can only be that Matilda wrote to Richard. She is aware of our adventures and contrives to put a stop to it all.'

'I know that you and she do not get on, but really Beth, Hilda is not the witch you think she is.'

'You will always defend her. You see not her poison as I do.' William pours some ale in my goblet. 'Aye, women, they never could shoot an arrow straight.'

Something has been on my mind that I must share. 'I fear Edward may soon return. What do you foresee will become of us?'

I see a change coming over him, an unusual pensiveness. He removes his cap from his head, allowing brown curls to fall loose and I resist the urge to run my fingers through them. He sighs, 'well, if he were to find out about us, he would have my guts for garters.'

I at once regret my questioning, for his mood has changed, as has mine, losing both appetite and desire. William rises and walks over to the great oak tree, leaning his back against it. 'Some things are better left unsaid Beth,' he says. 'I thought we were here only to share a little joy in our dreary lives, not to beget melancholy, for there is quite enough of that already.'

I rise to my feet and walk over to him. 'Forgive me William for my foolishness. As you are aware, I am disposed to allowing my feelings to over-rule all reason.'

William's warmth slowly returns, and he accepts me in his arms. 'Aye, you women are as unwieldy as stray horses.'

Chapter 14

Darkness is all consuming, yet it refuses to draw me into sleep. I sense people around me, yet I cannot see anything. Confused and disorientated, I reach out to get a feel of my surroundings, touching rough cold stone, which triggers my sight, and immediately I am aware of being in a large room dimly lit by candles fixed in iron holders that are attached to the walls. I notice tapestries and a magnificent fireplace heralded by an imposing coat of arms.

A small group of musicians are playing in a corner of the room and there appears to be an array of activity, with people, mainly ladies wearing beautiful gowns, milling about. Some are idly chatting; a small group are playing cards and an elderly couple are enjoying a board game. A man is quietly reading by the light of a small candle and servants are filling tankards on demand.

Then I become aware of the lady, very petite, perched on a ledge by a small window, toying with her very wide wedding band, which looks out of proportion and uncomfortable on her tiny fingers. She has on her usual blue gown with a collar of white fur, a gold circlet on top of her head and her long hair is draped in an ornate braid down her back. She appears sad and dreamy and I am drawn to study her more closely. As I approach, she turns her head and looks directly at me, then cries out as though she has seen a ghost, her eyes wide and wild. Simultaneously I too gasp in shock, for it is as if I am looking at myself.

Instantaneously I find I am back on my sofa. Raising myself up, I stare at the untouched mug of tea on the coffee table, slowly becoming aware of the television drone in the background. I have been a little sceptical of Mason's suggestion that the lady in my visions is another version of myself, even though I've noticed before that she looked a bit like me. This though, was the first time I got to look at her face properly, and having been confronted with a virtual mirror image, I'm beginning to wonder if he was right after-all.

Chapter 15

Usually, I retire to my chamber following dinner, but it is Kathryn's birthday and we are all at the behest of Matilda to partake in the soirée that she has arranged. We have left the great hall for the solar and on a bellyful of food, I desire only to sleep. I have little fervour for the company here and am not one for pretence, though this be a sword in my side. There is but one person of whom I would be with, but William and I must show prudence, imparting nothing more than an occasional glance to allay the gossip that I sense is already conjuring about us.

I am in audience with Kathryn and Eleanor, having to abide yet more prattling about the former's betrothed. All but she knows him for the rogue with two faces that he is, yet she refuses to hear ill of him. I am fond of Kathryn and have some sympathy, yet I find her gross naivety an irritation. My eyes rest on her mutt, as ever, nestled in her arms. The lazy creature is habitually asleep. The dull discourse ensues unbearably, and I find my eyes wandering about the room. The minstrels are tuning up and people take their seats for a game of cards. My eyes fix on William in audience with Matilda. I am familiar with his alluring tricks and watch as he performs them with her. She too plays a beguiling dance, using her eyes, her hair, a sudden touch to his arm.

Matilda sees me watching and smiles wickedly. She is known to enjoy courtly attention, yet I wonder if her play with William is contrived to vex me. I sigh, finding I can bear it no more, withdrawing myself to a window seat and looking out onto the cold dark night. I see the moon full and bright and begin to lose myself in its magnetic glare, blanking out my surroundings and drifting into a dream state.

My silence is disturbed by a sudden coldness, a slight draft drawing around me and a strange unquiet permeates the air. And as I turn back to the room I see a phantom right before my eyes, the haze of a lady standing looking directly at me.

I scream out and the image at once fades away, dissolving into the ether.

Chapter 16

I am in the kitchen preparing myself a sandwich when Margot breezes in, and, without a word, begins clearing up after me. She skulks about my house as if she owns the place and I never know when next she will creep up on me. I really must try to persuade Lawrence that we don't need her, that I would prefer to clean the house myself.

'It's four o'clock Margot,' I say, 'you must be finished for the day?'

'Nearly madam. I noticed that your friend left some of his clothes in your bedroom and didn't know if you wanted me to pop them in the laundry?'

'Oh, no don't worry. He had to stay over last night because he'd had too much to drink. I'll give them back to him.' I silently reproach myself for being so bloody careless, forgetting to tidy them up. She must know what is going on, she's not stupid, but at the end of the day it's none of her business.

James rings to say he'll be out with his mates tonight, so it looks like I'll be on my own. It'll be a good opportunity for some *me* time. My leg has been seizing up all day, so I prop it up with cushions, turn off the tv and put on a cd of timeless ballads that lulls me into a daydream. As I take a sip of wine, for a brief odd moment, it appears I am drinking from a goblet, rather than my glass.

The music takes me back to my first date with Lawrence, the perfect gentleman, greeting me with a bunch of white roses at Cobbleyard's, the most expensive restaurant in town. We had met the day before at my friend Tanya's wedding, an instant attraction for us both. We married just four months later after a whirlwind courtship, a small affair in a registry office. I realised early on that it had all been too soon, that we didn't know each other well enough, and things started rapidly to go downhill. It is hard to know why things changed so quickly, but Lawrence's heavy drinking is undoubtedly a factor, although he would never admit it. Each day I would wonder whether I'd be waking up to nice or nasty Lawrence, as he tends to alternate from being loving to tyrannical. He uses me as a punchbag when he's unstable and I am tired of walking on egg shells, being jittery and insecure. The relief of him going away steered me recklessly into the arms of James, an attractive man who rekindled my flame. Feeling deprived of love, he filled the void, and now I am addicted.

But where does the future lie? In all honesty we haven't been together for long enough to know if things will lead anywhere. My thoughts on James are ambiguous, for as much as I'd like to think of him as my knight in shining armour, my gut says that he is a non-committal guy. He tends to steer clear of any conversation about Lawrence and refuses to talk about the future. He is younger than me and quite immature, is on a meagre wage and shares a rented house with students. I have a great lifestyle and a lot to lose materially and yet I can't say I am happy. I just can't make up my mind what I want, whether to end it all with Lawrence, as everyone advises, or to give it another shot. Perhaps things will be different when he returns, that absence really does make the heart grow fonder.

My thoughts are interrupted by my mobile. It's Rosa. 'Hi, why don't you come down and join us all? It's Eva's birthday and we're having a bit of a ding-dong.' She sounds quite drunk. I hesitate, 'well, I'm all comfy here.'

'Oh, don't be so bloody boring. Get your arse down here,' she says, and the phone goes dead.

I um and ah for a-while, then decide it may not be such a bad idea after-all; anything to keep my thoughts from going in ever increasing circles.

I am greeted by Rosa, so drunk that she nearly falls over. 'Come on Gracie, Eva's put on a barrel, come and join the troops. Where's Jimmy?'

'Who?'

'Oh sorry, *James*,' she emphasizes his name in a posh voice etched with sarcasm.

'Please Rosa, keep your voice down. I don't want everyone to know about us.'

'Oh, don't be such a prude. If you honestly think you can keep a secret at the Laughing Pig, you're crazy. So where is he anyway?'

'He's at the Green Hen with his mates.' Rosa pulls an exaggerated sad face and saunters off.

Mason approaches laughing. 'She's a bit worse for wear,' he says.

'Yes, she does like her alcohol.' He buys me a drink and we wander outside where it's quieter to talk. 'So, how have things been, have you had any more visions?'

'Not since we spoke yesterday, when she and I made eye contact. That was weird, but I wonder now if it was all just a dream.'

'So, ok, do you feel any more at ease about it all now?'

'Well, I'm still trying to assimilate what you said about simultaneous lives and time distortion,' I laugh. 'It all freaks me out a bit, but I really appreciate you helping me.'

'Well, I'm not suggesting that I know what's going on any more than you do Grace because what you have described is highly unusual to say the least. I'm merely offering a possible explanation. Have you ever tried meditation?'

'Err no, I don't think I'd be any good at it.'

He lights his roll-up. 'I think it would be good for you. I can teach you if you like?'

My mobile rings, it's James. 'Hi Babes, just wondered if I could come over? I could do with a snuggle.'

'Well, I'm at the Laughing Pig, why don't you come and join us? It's Eva's birthday; free drinks.'

When James arrives, Rosa makes a bee-line for him. She throws her arms around his neck before I even get a look-in. 'Jimmy darling, I'm so glad you came.' I begin to feel a little unsteady as a blurriness forms before my eyes. I know what is occurring but can't stop it, watching as Rosa takes on the persona of the shady mistress of the castle, then reverts back just as quickly. I watch her wrapped around James, whispering something in his ear and my body shivers as they look too intimate for comfort.

Chapter 17

'I may not believe that in a room full of people, I was the only one to see the phantom. Do you think it is pursuing me?'

'Well Matilda thinks you are fantasising. She says there have never been any reports of phantoms here, other than what you appear to have seen,' William says.

'I would deem that to be unlikely in a castle as old as this. And what thinks she, this friend of yours; that I am utterly mad?'

'This friend of mine is actually my cousin madam and she presumes that you are inclined to court attention,' he says with some irritation.

I gasp, 'and I suppose you agree with your cousin?'

'I know not what you expect Beth, when you are so disposed to making a fool of yourself.' He rudely mounts his horse and rides away leaving me behind, quite alone and woeful.

I summon Tenwyn, for he has a method of comforting me in a way that only he can. 'I may not rest the blame of the apparition on your potion, for I have ceased to take it. The visions were becoming too much, and my sleeping has in any case been a little better of late.'

Tenwyn toys with his beard contemplatively. 'That is good news indeed, Elizabeth.'

'I know I am not the most affable person, but I fear I have not a friend in the world right now,' I say, fiddling with my wedding band, a habit of mine when I am troubled.

Master Tenwyn draws closer. 'Ah, come now, I am your friend,' he says warmly. 'Beneath your haughtiness you are as soft and supple as a lady's glove.' He pours wine into two goblets, offering one to me. His kindness brings tears to my eyes, which I wipe away hurriedly, straightening my back to regain self-control.

Tenwyn returns to his seat. 'Pray tell me more of this phantom.' He sits quietly stroking his beard.

'It was brief and not all that clear, but I saw the lady that I have seen before with un-braided hair and strange attire. She was standing before me, just staring.' I shudder at the memory. 'Master Tenwyn, how may I put a stop to this haunting? Why is this lady after me and nobody else?' I notice Henriette falters at her task of laying fresh rushes on the floor and methinks she is eavesdropping again. 'You are dismissed,' I say in a commanding voice to make her aware that I am addressing her. 'You may resume later.' She drops the rushes in surprise, failing to conceal a natural petulance.

William waits until she leaves. 'Well unfortunately we are talking about forces beyond our control Lady Elizabeth. It is noteworthy that you alone saw her, which would suggest that she may have an association with you. Is she familiar in any way, perhaps someone on the other side of the veil?'

'No sir, not that I am aware of, although she is mayhap a little like me.'

'And so your sleep is more restful now?'

'Well, with all the recent comings and goings, I have been quite overcome with exhaustion, hence having no need of the potion. Though last night I had a nightmare, which caused me to scream out, scaring the very life out of my maid.' I smile at the memory of her distress.

'Do you remember what story it told?'

'Not a great deal. I recall only being chased on my horse, frozen with fear as would be a deer on a hunt. I believe sir it was caused by the disquiet brought forth by my husband's command to cast aside my horse. I vow it shall not happen. Pharaoh is my redeemer.'

'Yet your husband may insist on it when he returns.'

'Well, that shall be a matter to contend with then. His home-coming fills me with angst, for he is quite a heartless man.'

Master Tenwyn searches for something in his bag. 'Here is a potion for the melancholy, that shall assist in upraising your spirits. Mix it with a little ale at sun-up and sun-down, for the taste and smell does revolt the senses, but it is made by my dear lady wife with most potent herbs.'

I smile. 'You sir are the only person who understands me.' Ever the gentleman, he smiles, bowing his head reverently and departs.

William is brooding, as he does not summon my company for the ride the next day, even though the sky is clear with sunshine. Hence, I decide that I shall go alone, despite the marshal's misgivings. 'These lands are not fit for unchaperoned ladies. They are perilous, with rocks hidden beneath the long grass,' he says gruffly.

'I am no stranger to them Master Hedyn and neither is my horse,' I reply indignantly.

'Let my lad accompany you, my lady.'

'Pray no, I am quite capable without company.'

I hear laughter behind me. 'Aye and a stubborn mule at that. Prepare my horse and I shall accompany the lady, whether she likes it or not,' William chuckles wryly. I am surprised and privately gladdened at his unexpected presence, though I shall not permit to show it, tutting and turning my back on him instead. We ride out to our usual spot and the freshness of the air raises my spirits. William helps me down from Pharaoh and draws me to him. Never mind Tenwyn's tonics. I vow that, in this moment in time, a ride out with Pharaoh and William is all that I desire.

Chapter 18

Caesar twitches his ears, pleased to see me. I often wonder if he understands why I have not ridden him since the accident. 'I'm not being fair to you boy, am I?' I say, fondly slapping his shiny black shoulder. 'Don't worry, I promise you, no one will ever take you away from me. How about we get you down to the riding school so that you can take children out for rides? I'll still come and see you each day, and as soon as I get my strength and confidence back, we will go riding again.'

He looks at me with his huge black eyes and I detect his impatience, willing me to stop talking and get on with feeding him. It is a little chilly today, so I throw the rug over his back before setting him out to graze and stand at the fence watching him eagerly chewing the dewy grass. A recollection of a recent vision comes to mind of my medieval lady riding out with her lover and them settling down to a picnic beneath a huge tree. Their horses waited patiently under another tree, hers a magnificent dapple grey of similar to height to Caesar, and his, a chestnut, slightly smaller.

My right leg begins to hurt, so I start back across the sprawling lawns to the house. Gerald the gardener is busy pruning the roses and I stop to ask if he would like a cup of tea. 'No thanks my lovely, I always bring a flask and sandwiches with me,' he says. I am just about to ask him about a tree on the far side of the garden, when I see Margot at the back door calling me, waving the phone in her hand. I make my way back as quickly as is possible with a stiff leg and she hands me the phone, but when I answer it, the person has hung off.

'It was your husband madam,' she says.

'Oh, ok thanks, I'm sure he'll phone back.' Predictably there are five missed calls from him on my mobile, along with a voicemail that I won't bother to listen to. When he next rings I will get the usual badgering about not carrying my phone around with me at all times. 'It's called a mobile phone for a reason,' is his mantra. I think back to our conversation last night when he spoke of his plans for our future, as though we are a normal happy couple. He said he wants us to go on a cruise around the Med and spoke again about us applying for IVF treatment. But I am haunted by memories of that fateful night before he left, when we had a row, and he bent my wrist behind me so hard I thought it would snap. Then he pushed me violently against the bedroom door and as I fought back, he hit me in the face, producing a swollen black eye that took ages to heal. The row started over his lost keys, then escalated when I confronted him about his drinking. I should have known better to address this when he was already drunk.

The next day he demanded an apology from me that I had driven him too far and he is so damned clever and manipulative that, at the time, he made me feel that indeed I was wholly to blame for his violence. Now, in the cold light of day, I take responsibility for provoking him, but the rest lies with him. I feel a line was crossed that night and I wonder if life can ever be the same with him again, now that I know just what he is capable of.

Chapter 19

'I pray you my lady to take heed, for falsehoods and gossip are rife here,' Master Tenwyn says, as he sups from his goblet. He has become a light in this dark pit of a castle, the only one who understands me and who tolerates my whimsical tendencies and indiscretions.

'Falsehood and gossip?' I laugh. 'Master Tenwyn, this is and has always been, practice within a castle's walls. What else may the delicate ladies speak of when their needlework threads have run out? Amusement is derived from drama, even though much of it be concocted.' I am still laughing, yet his expression remains sober.

'Indeed, yet gossip may also be perilous. I fear you shall be wounded by Sir William's blunt sword and as your faithful servant and friend, this troubles me. The man has no honour and the path you tread may lead only to strife.' He inclines his head, sensing that he may have ventured too far.

I find myself discouraged that gossip has brought to him news of my dalliance with William. Tenwyn goes on. 'I am sorry to say that he is a dog forever on the prowl for fresh bones, before even savouring the ones that he already has.'

'What are you suggesting Master Tenwyn? Sir William and I are very good friends. He has been aiding me with my wayward horse and riding out with me. There may be no harm in that.'

'As you will,' he sighs, 'but pray remember that I am gifted with my family's heritage to see what others may not. Sir William shall bring poison to your door. My duty is not to meddle, but to serve and protect you.'

All of a sudden, I feel befuddled and my vision becomes hazy and when I glance at Tenwyn, he looks different.

He rises from his chair. 'Are you alright my lady?'

'You... well you looked different for a moment.' I shake my head. 'It was one of my funny turns again. Really, what am I to do?'

Tenwyn rests his hand on my shoulder and I feel a warm current from it. 'There is nothing there to fear,' he says gently. 'You are merely glimpsing beyond the veil.'

Chapter 20

I feel as if I've known Mason for years. His pale blue eyes contrast with his dark hair and there is a sense of depth and mystery about him that intrigues me. I find it surprising that he doesn't have a girlfriend, but perhaps he is too out of the ordinary for a lot of women. I watch with amusement as he removes the cushion from behind him before sinking back into the leather armchair. For some reason cushions are a thing that some men just aren't comfortable with.

'How are you getting on with James?' he asks.

'Ok,' I respond, 'why do you ask?'

'It's just a gut feeling. There's something about him.'

'You and your gut feelings. Have you always been like that?'

'Intuitive?' he chuckles. 'It's in my blood, we're all crazy in my family. My mum teaches mediumship. Gran is psychic too, but she learned to keep it all to herself because she didn't want to end up in a mental home like her mother.'

I clear my throat. 'You must think I'm a tart carrying on with James, me being a married woman.'

'Albeit an unhappy one. Look, I am not going to judge what you do, but I think he is using you and I don't want to see you get hurt.'

I feel defensive, 'I don't think that's fair. James is easily misunderstood, but his hearts in the right place.'

I laugh to see froth pouring forth onto his jeans as he opens a can of beer. 'Just be careful Grace. I think you're playing with fire,' he says as he mops his jeans with his hand.

'I know,' I relinquish. 'I just have to get my head in gear. My life is a mess.' I start to nervously chew on my nail then think better of it. 'I got some pills from the doctor today. I've been putting off going, but felt I needed something to calm my nerves and also help me to sleep. I explained about the nightmares and visions and he wanted to sign me up for counselling, but I don't want to go down that road.'

'What did he give you, tranquilisers?'

'Yes.'

Be careful Grace, they will dull your senses and turn you into a zombie. It's much better to deal with things head-on. Don't be afraid of your visions. You should learn to accept them and then they won't seem like a threat. I would be careful who you talk to about these things as well, especially that husband of yours. I don't know him, but he sounds like the sort of bloke who would have you sectioned. Like I said, people don't understand these things.'

'I know you're right Mason. I just want to be normal,' I sigh, reaching for the packet of cigarettes on the table.

'I didn't know you smoked.'

'I used to and have started again recently, albeit only a few a day. When I think about it, I am doing everything Lawrence hates; drinking, smoking, having a social life, being unfaithful...'

We go outside to the patio and light up. 'Ditch the pills,' says Mason inhaling deeply. 'I know you're sceptical, but trust me, meditation will be a whole lot more helpful.'

Just then I hear the trill of my mobile from the living room. I rush in to get it, but it stops just as I pick it up. Surprise, surprise, it was Lawrence.

And then the door opens and in walks James.

Chapter 21

As I enter the solar, a hush fills the room suggesting that I am gossip of the day. The ladies seated in their usual circle with their heads down, diligently work away with their needles. Oh, the tedium of castle life! Matilda, adorned in her sumptuous red gown, looks up in feigned surprise. 'Oh Elizabeth, to what do we owe the pleasure of your company, when it strikes me you prefer the comradeship of country gentlemen to us fair women folk?'

Her provocative words yield giggles and snide glances amongst my fair women folk. I select a chemise that is for repair from the basket, refusing to reply and yet she probes deeper. 'Are you not riding out with William on such a fine day?'

'It would seem not since I am here with my fair women folk,' I retort.

'Oh, I hear he was whiling the night away at the taverns again last night. It is no wonder he is today unfit for the saddle,' quips Elowen. Kathryn gasps, causing her skittish mutt to jump from her lap. 'Surely a gentleman like William would not frequent such places?' she says in surprise.

'What William does is nobody's affair but his own,' I reply, with as much composure as I am able to muster, though secretly I am uneasy as her words resonate with Tenwyn's misgivings. It is unthinkable that William may be whoring in the taverns, then coming to me in rabid lust. Today is the *second time this week that he has pulled from the ride. Could it be his interest in me is waning?*

Matilda seeks to further goad me. 'Have you seen your phantom again?' she enquires to further snickers. I decide not to respond lest I go too far, for I would verily slap her priggish face.

'My dear,' she pursues, 'you look so pale and thin. I ought to arrange a new physician for you. For someone who spends so much time at your side, Master Tenwyn appears to be doing so little for your frail disposition. He is little more than a Cornish charmer.'

I prick my finger in temper, throwing the chemise to the ground. 'Pray, refrain from your meddling Matilda, for I am quite well and Tenwyn meets my requests without faulter or flaw.' I take hold of my skirts, tainted with blood from my finger and charge from the solar, leaving behind gasps and chatter. Arriving back at my own chamber I sit, then as soon as I have regained my breath, I command Henriette to summon Master Tenwyn.

I am kept waiting for a long time since he has been called to attend on somebody else. When he eventually arrives, Henriette serves him a goblet of wine, then positions herself on a stool in the corner of the room. I am still fired up and dismiss her crossly. Tenwyn is right when he warns of the servants. She is one that I most certainly do not trust. As ever, his presence has a quieting effect on me, and I unleash on him my tales of woe. He looks at me with wise eyes. 'Like I have said before, the walls have ears. I may offer you a potion, but methinks that there would be more to gain from the comfort of a friend,' he smiles.

'You are right Tenwyn, for I am quite friendless here, even though I am aware I have brought much to my own door. I ...'

We are interrupted by William charging in, rudely unannounced. His hair and clothes are unkempt, and it is evident that he has imbibed in too much ale. Tenwyn rises and bows his head slightly in deference. William gives him a look of flagrant displeasure. 'What is he doing here?' he asks bluntly.

I stand, raising my head haughtily, concealing my alarm at his appearance and insolence. 'This is my physician, Master Tenwyn,' I say.

'I know who he is, but what is he doing here?' Tenwyn glances at me and I nod to dismiss him. He collects his cap and bows to us both, then moves towards the door, but instead of departing, he stands there protectively like a guard, reluctant to leave me alone with this drunkard. William swivels on his foot and commands 'go man, go!' Tenwyn looks at me and I nod at him again with a smile and watch him reluctantly leave.

William belches loudly, shocking me with his uncouthness. 'I do not like that man,' he says. 'He should know his place and you madam are far too familiar with him,' he says pointing his finger at me.

'Do not presume you may burst into my chamber and dismiss my guests, sir! Master Tenwyn is a most worthy gentleman. Indeed, there is rumour about the sort of company that you choose to keep!'

'Really madam, you and your team of chamber ladies have nothing better to do than spread churlish slander. This place is oppressive and the company here is tiresome. Goodbye madam.'

He storms off leaving me in shock. I sit and toy with my wedding band, noticing the blood stains dotted all over my beautiful gown and find myself welling up with bitter angry tears. And I find myself weeping out aloud. The last time I cried so was when my beloved palfrey died as a child.

Chapter 22

James ambles in and pecks me on the cheek. 'Hi, you're early,' I say, irritated at the sound of my mobile ringing again. 'Mason's outside having a fag, why don't you go and join him?' I say. He responds with a sultry look and loud belch, as I pace to the kitchen to answer the call. Lawrence is questioning our credit card bill, wanting to know what I have been buying. It's true that I have recently invested in a few new clothes since my social life has sparked up again, but I always keep within my monthly budget. Despite the fact that he is on a great salary, he likes to keep me on a tight rein. I try aimlessly to defend myself, but he is having none of it. 'I can see there are going to be some changes when I get home,' he says before hanging up.

On venturing back into the living room, James is standing alone cracking open a beer. 'Where is Mason?' I ask, looking around.

'Gone,' he says nonchalantly. 'I don't know why you hang around with him, he's an arsehole.'

'Because he is a very good friend of mine,' I say with my hands on my hips. 'Did you say something to him?'

'Didn't have to,' he belches then chuckles at his own private joke. 'What did Lawrence want this time?'

'Mind your own business. I really don't need this. You'll have to leave. I want a quiet night in!' James looks surprised at my outburst. 'Why, what have I done?' I wonder if I may have over-reacted, but I have had it up to here with the men in my life.

'Please James, just give me some space. I've had a hard day.'

'Typical! Your husband pisses you off and you take it out on me.' He grabs his jacket and leaves.

'Why do I always screw things up?' I ask out loud, fetching my coat and taking a bottle of wine and cigarettes out with me to the garden.

A combination of blinding panic and driving rain lashing against my face obscures all my senses. I shorten the reins and use my heels to urge the horse on faster, hearing shouts and taunts from uncouth men closing in on me. A part of me knows that I am dreaming, and I manage to jolt myself awake, sweating, breathless and relieved, but can't help but wonder why it keeps on recurring. James tends to stay over less now, fed up with being woken by me shouting out in my sleep or kicking him. I can't say I blame him, although it is hard to shrug off a feeling of being used when he leaves straight after our love making.

My head is pounding, so I get up for some painkillers. It is only five o'clock in the morning, but I doubt I'll manage to get back to sleep now, so I splash cold water on my face to wake myself up. As I raise my head to look at my reflection in the mirror, I jump at the sight. For it is not me who I see, but the woman of my visions. Whilst our features are a close match, her countenance reflects a very different personality to my own. I gasp and the vision fades, revealing my own reflection, eyes wide and mouth ajar.

Chapter 23

The grey clouds promise rain today, so I shall not be riding out. Neither do I desire to join the dreary company of the ladies in the solar. It is far more interesting to watch from my seat at the window the bustling comings and goings of castle life. I observe a small group of guards enamoured of a milkmaid, brushing past them wantonly swishing her skirts and smiling, undoubtedly courting crude remarks. A cart is being unloaded of yet more wood for the fires, which in some parts of the castle are ever burning now as the cold season sets in, and yet there is rarely warmth here save for feast nights. I spot a messenger in the distance making his way down the long winding road, conceivably bearing correspondence from our men, which would proffer no joy for me, since Edward's letters are usually brought about by someone's malice here. On the horizon, men are at work in the fields with their scythes, gathering hay. I draw my shawl tighter about my shoulders as a sharp breeze enters the narrow window.

There has been no sign of William today and neither am I in any mood to see him after the way he conducted himself towards my good friend Tenwyn. I think that I must be quite foolish to have fallen for his guiles. I have observed his dalliances with the ladies here, smiling and quipping, watching them reveiling in his attentions like hungry salivating pups. Indeed, I am surprised to have been the object of his desire amongst such a basket of delights, though I am wise to the fact that this has brought jealousy to my door. It is difficult to believe that a gentleman such as he, may have been frequenting the local taverns seeking succour from wanton women, and yet I am fully aware of his tendency to recklessness. It would seem I lost all sensibility to have nurtured an affection for such a man; a drunken rogue. I know it may not prevail, for such a course would be disastrous. I shudder to even contemplate the consequences. And yet, despite all, I may not fool myself that I do not miss the revelry that we shared, the rides out, his quipping and, most of all, his loving attentions.

My thoughts are interrupted by Henriette bringing in fresh rushes for the floor. Behind her is Father Arthur, the castle's chaplain. 'Pardon the intrusion my lady, if this is a bad time?'

'No, not at all Father, pray take a seat.' Henriette places the brushes in a corner and makes it her duty to bring ale for our guest. She knows her job well enough, yet it is her brooding petulance which lets her down.

'To what do I owe the pleasure of your company sir?'

'There are concerns about you Elizabeth, about your health and disposition, notwithstanding your recent absence from chapel, which has not gone unnoticed.'

'Oh 'tis nothing but poor sleep that has kept me abed for too long, as well as a touch of seasonal melancholy sir.'

Father Arthur is of a sombre disposition. He is a small round, yet imposing man. I feel like his little dark eyes are capable of burrowing deep into my soul. 'Is it true that you have been seeing things; that you believe the castle is haunted?'

I know how superstitious the Cornish folk are and my senses caution me of heeding my words to a priest such as he, for he may be disposed to believe I am bedevilled by demons or such the like. 'Nay sir,' I laugh nervously. 'My sight is poor within these castle walls. The shadows from the candles play tricks with the mind you know. I ever was accused of having an over-active imagination.'

He does not look convinced. 'Might I suggest you make the effort to attend chapel regularly my lady, for it is the best potion for troubled minds? Do not underestimate the necessity of the absolution, for a vacuum may become a gateway for the darkness to intrude.' He rises, summoning me to follow suit, then placing his hand upon my head, chants a Latin recital, little of which I can understand, as Latin was never my strong point, though I can determine enough that it is a prayer for the sick. He crosses himself and I follow suit. Then he makes to leave with the words 'just remember, the Lord saves us from ourselves.'

'Indeed. Thank you, Father.' As he departs my chamber, I feel myself shudder as he seems to leave behind shadows of menacing whispers.

I recall Tenwyn's words of caution. 'The walls have ears.' There is nowhere to hide and nowhere to run. There are ghouls and shadows at every turn.

Chapter 24

'It was scary Mason, because I saw her in the mirror, and it was a bit like looking at myself ... and yet it wasn't. It's difficult to explain.'

'Yes, because she is, or was, another version of you. Remember what I told you about past lives and that time is an illusion. You seem to be witnessing this *you* from another time, but on a parallel level. Stop shaking your head,' he laughs. 'I know it all sounds crazy, but Grace this is happening, and you need to do something about it. You have a choice, you can be the victim or put all your conditioning aside, accept it and start taking charge. I am a strong believer that everything happens for a reason. My grandmother always said to me, *don't try to control or fight the tide; become it*. Ok, lecture over.' He smiles and I realise I have just witnessed another side to him, a passion that contrasts with his usual laid-back demeanour.

'You are right,' I sigh 'and I am so lucky to have you as a friend Mason. I'm just not sure how to take charge though. Can you help me?'

'Ok, so, if you have the right mind-set, you're halfway there. Your dreams and visions are telling you something, so begin to observe them as the interesting events that they are and keep a record, so that you can start to piece it all together. It's important to compartmentalize, to keep them separate from everyday life, and you don't want this other version of you to over-shadow your own personality as Grace.' He pauses for breath, quietly delving into his thoughts. 'I'm going to teach you to meditate, which will serve to calm your nerves and help you gain a more spiritual perspective. But also, we can use a technique using an imaginary mirror as a metaphor to focus in on this other time, so that you are in charge of the visions, as opposed to the other way around.'

Mason patiently takes me through the techniques step by step, leading me eventually into a deep peaceful trance-like state. When it is time to come back to the room I resist momentarily, wanting to stay in this safe comforting place. Then slowly I open my eyes and stretch out my arms with a huge yawn. 'Wow that was so relaxing. Did you just hypnotize me?'

'Well, I took you into a deep meditation, but both are altered states of consciousness, and therefore, closely linked. Remember, meditation takes practice and patience. Just try to be disciplined and incorporate it into your daily routine.'

'Alright, I will. I was wondering about something though. What if we've got it all wrong, that this other person isn't me? Maybe she is a ghost haunting me?'

'Well, you said yourself that she looks like you and don't forget you are able to recognize people you know now, in the other lifetime.'

'Yes, you being one of them, the doctor figure. Strange really, because you are a bit like a doctor to me now,' I giggle.

Walking into the pub later with James, I notice Rosa and Eva sitting at a table in the corner and Eva appears to be crying. James makes his way to the bar and I go to find out what's going on. As Eva sobs into her beer, Rosa explains that her fiancé's ex-girlfriend is back in town and they have been seeing each-other behind Eva's back. For a split second as I watch her cry, I catch a flash memory of a lady from my visions but am not able to recollect it at this time, so I make a mental note to write it down when I get home, as per Mason's instructions.

I place my hand on Eva's shoulder saying, 'I'm so sorry Eva, I'm sure he will come to his senses,' knowing all the while how feeble this sounds, but it's difficult to know what words to use. She blows her nose and rises from the table. 'I must look a sight. I need to go and clean up, then get back to the bar to help poor Lizzie.' She walks away bravely, and James arrives with the drinks. Rosa throws her arms around him with a big smile, saying 'Hello Jimmy!' She turns to me. 'He is such a hard taskmaster you know. You should see the way he gets me running around that tennis court. I've never ached so much in my life.'

James chuckles, 'I haven't got a reputation for nothing,' he says. I observe the mirrored body language of he and Rosa and wonder what reputation he is referring to. For the rest of the evening I watch them both out the corner of my eye, left in no doubt of the flirting going on between them. Rosa is giving him all the signs, wide eyed smiles, the odd casual touch to his arm, laughing at his ridiculous jokes. James is lapping it all up and they are both caught up in their own little world, while I feel invisible, like I'm on the outside looking in. After a-while, I can take it no more. I collect my coat and make the long walk home. It is forty-five minutes by the time James has noticed me missing, ringing me finally. 'Where are you?' he asks.

'At home. I didn't think you would notice me gone, you were so wrapped up in Rosa's company.'

'Are you serious? Can't I speak to a friend of the opposite sex?'

'James, do you have any idea of Rosa's reputation? She sleeps with anyone she chooses.'

'But she's your friend.'

'Precisely.' I hang up. He might be naive, but I am not. I have seen Rosa in action before. She sets her target and goes for it; single, taken, married or whatever, and the men always fall for it because she is attractive, and they are flattered, simple as that.

But to do this to me, her friend?

Chapter 25

Matilda has invited nobility from all around to celebrate her birthday with a banquet. Ever one for setting out to make an impression, she has employed more minstrels to add to her small band, along with singers, a jester, and a group of players for entertainment.

Other than attending chapel for fear of affirming Father Arthur's suspicions, I have spent the past two days in my chamber choosing not to see anyone, for it would seem that I am under close scrutiny at every turn. Never before have I witnessed the great hall so full. I feel quite alone amongst so many guests, and I have few friends. Therefore, I am gladdened to see Kathryn approaching, though she appears forlorn. I think this must be the only occasion I have seen her without the mutt in her arms. When I ask what troubles her, she bursts into tears and I quickly usher her away from the great hall, free from prying eyes and poisoned tongues, into a small antechamber. 'Pray, what troubles you Kat?' I hand her my kerchief.

'It is Henry,' she says. My hand aches for writing to him, yet I have had no reply for some time. And I am privy to hearsay of his infidelity, that he is enamoured of another. When he returns from battle, it is said that he intends to nullify our contract.' Her face resembles a deer waiting to be struck by the arrow. 'Have you heard anything Beth?' Her expression seems to implore that I tell her what she has heard is false, yet it pains me that I may not.

I place my hand upon her shoulder. 'My dear, it is true. It has been spoken of for some time.' She cries out and I bid her to sit, beckoning a servant to bring her a goblet of wine.

'Then why am I the last to know? She beseeches. 'Why is everyone so friendless that none of these whispers have reached my own ears? Is there anyone who is faithful in this place? Why indeed has not Henry spoken of this to me, rather than conspiring behind closed doors?' Her sorrow has turned to rage. She picks up her skirts and hastens from the room. I am aggrieved for my friend, cognizant myself of being at the behest of heartless men.

At the sound of trumpets heralding the guests to the tables, I make my way back to the great hall. Everyone looks resplendent in their best refinery. Music plays merrily in the background and great trays of food are arriving at the long tables. Such display is most costly in these harsh times and I wonder if grandeur would be approved of by my brother Richard, Matilda's husband. I believe he would be outraged at such indulgence.

Everyone is making their way to their appointed places. Matilda has positioned me next to William on one side and Tenwyn the other, as if I have been employed for the evening's amusement. Is my lady hostess baiting me before setting the wolves free? I look over to her seated on the dais, catching her eye. She smiles at me with cunning and conceit and I stare back at her icily. It is she who plots to take my horse from me, pits my husband against me, then sends the castle's chaplain to my door with the accusation that I am mad or bedevilled. And now she incites more rumour against me by positioning me between my rogue lover and most trusted friend for all eyes to see.

William addresses me with false charm. 'Lady Beth, how good it is to see you. I thought you had hidden yourself away?'

'No sir, I merely sought a little refuge from bad company,' I retort. I am in no mood for idle chat and I shall be no charade. I will eat, sharing neither words nor expression, then retire to my chamber.

The following day Tenwyn comes to visit me. 'You appeared troubled last night,' he says.

'Indeed, I have been sir, with the castle's chaplain set upon me with his threatening sermons, atop of washer-women's tittle-tattle and Sir William's disgraceful behaviour. I have been seeing strange things that are neither here nor there, and my sleep is disturbed by phantoms and dreams. My husband may return at any moment and the lord only knows what may happen then.' I have worked myself up into a distraught stupor. Tenwyn comes and takes my hands in his to compose me. I become aware of Henriette standing in the corner watching and listening like a hawk intent on its prey, and glare at her, watching her quickly retreat.

'Pray be calm,' Tenwyn says. 'Gossip shall always abound in these places. You should not confine yourself to your room. Go about your daily business with your head held high to allay any suspicions and be sure to keep your own counsel. Folk will soon stop gossiping about you and move onto the next suspecting prey. If you stay in your chamber, you will just add more fuel to the fire.'

'You are 'ere the voice of reason Tenwyn,' I say, feeling a little calmer now.

'And pray, heed my warnings of Sir William. Now I am going to give you a little potion to settle your disposition and help you to rest.'
 'Rest sir, pray what is that?'

Chapter 26

'So why aren't you eating properly? You've hardly touched your food,' says James. I look across the table at him, admiring his well chiselled features and dark eyes.

'I don't know, there's just a lot going on in my head at the moment,' I say, half-heartedly twisting spaghetti onto my fork.

'You're getting skinny,' he remarks. He may be good looking, but he seriously lacks diplomacy. 'What was all that about the other night when you stormed out the pub?'

I look at him earnestly. 'I was upset because you and Rosa were flirting. But then I am married, so have no right to be jealous, have I, because I should never have got into this in the first place?' I say bitterly, giving up on my food and taking a large swig of wine.

'Oh thanks,' he says. 'So, you've just been using me.'

I refrain from saying the words on the tip of my tongue, that to me, it feels like it's the other way around. 'I'm sorry, I really enjoy being with you James. I didn't mean it like that, it's just that my conscience gets the better of me at times. I'm not like Rosa, I don't sleep around and, believe it or not, I did take my vows seriously on my wedding day.'

'Oh, I was wondering when you were going to mention the "R" word. You know how she flirts, she's like it with all the men. It doesn't mean that I'm going to sleep with her.'

'Trust me, I know when Rosa means business. She's not exactly being a good friend, behaving the way she does.'

James raises his glass to the waitress to fetch him another pint and an alarm bell ring in my head as he is already quite drunk. Hearing his phone beep, he removes it from his pocket, chuckling as he reads the message, then sends a text back to the sender, a smug grin on his face. I am irritated that someone has stolen his attention from our important conversation. I would like to see mobile phones banned from restaurants as I find them both rude and intrusive at a table setting.

'What's so funny?' I ask.

'Just a dirty joke.'

'Oh, who from?'

A pause. 'Rosa.'

James instantly detects my annoyance. 'Oh, for goodness sake, it's just a text.' He shakes his head stuffing a fork load of chips in his mouth. Another beep sounds and I watch him smile as he checks the message.

'Another one?' I ask. He nods his head.

'Ok, so if you want to spend the rest of the evening with me, I suggest you turn the damn thing off,' I say angrily. He puts the phone back in his pocket sulkily and carries on eating. The evening seemed to start out well enough, but now it is deteriorating rapidly, and my spirits are sinking fast. I look at James, wondering how best to salvage things, when my vision begins to cloud over, and I find myself confronted with the face of the lady in blue's secret lover. His features are similar to James's, but he has a fuller head of hair and a trim beard. But just as soon as I begin to focus on the image, it disappears, and I am faced back with a crabby James.

I remember what Mason told me to do in a crisis, become aware of my feet on the ground and take three long slow deep breaths. Feeling slightly better, I appeal to James. 'Look I know how pathetic this sounds, but do you have any feelings for me?'

'Of-course I do,' he says but refuses to look at me. His phone beeps again, but this time he ignores it.

I gaze despondently at my plate still laden with unwanted spaghetti. 'Ok, but do you just see me as a casual shag until hubby returns?' Talk of the devil, my own phone starts ringing and when I check, it is him. I cut him off straight away, turn my phone off and shove it back in my handbag.

'Look,' says James and this time we are interrupted by the waitress collecting our plates. We decline the dessert menu and wait until she has gone. James tries again. 'All this is beginning to get heavy. I mean, we've only been together a few weeks and you're killing the fun out of it. Why can't we just live for the moment, rather than worrying about the future all the chuffing time? It's such a passion killer.' He reaches his hand over the table gently clasping hold of my own, bringing charm to his eyes and I find my resolve melting away.

Little over an hour later we are in the throes of passion on my bed, when my mobile rings out from across the room. James swears and tells me to leave it, but I know that it will be Lawrence, and it would not do to incite his anger further since I ignored him earlier. James curses as I get up, rushing to retrieve the phone from under the pile of clothes, apologising and promising to be as quick as I can.

But when I get back ten minutes later, James is lying on his back snoring loudly.

The night has not been particularly productive, other than to fall into bed with each other, yet even that didn't work out well. I am still none the wiser about our relationship and neither do I trust Rosa. I find myself tossing and turning, unable to sleep, so end up in the living room with a cup of tea flicking through the channels on tv, but gambling sites and violent films do nothing for me, so I turn it off. Then I spot the candle on the coffee table that Mason gave me to help me meditate and decide to give it a go.

I sit for several minutes trying out the exercises he had prescribed, but no matter how hard I try, my mind starts conjuring thoughts, sabotaging my efforts. In the end I quit, cuddling up on the sofa into my blanket, easing myself into relaxation. I suddenly remember the mirror James told me to focus on and try to create an image in my mind. I can visualise it quite clearly, old fashioned in style, long and oval with ornate gold etching all the way around. James's instructions were to set the intention of viewing the other lifetime and then to focus on the mirror, but in a relaxed way.

What transpires is similar to when I experience visions, whereby initial haziness is succeeded by a sudden clarity. I see my lady being helped by her servant to dress in a sumptuous gown of royal blue, adorned with a gold braided y-shaped belt trailing to the ground and overly-long draped sleeves bedecked with the same braiding. The usual gold circlet sits on top of her head and unusual for her, her hair is loose and very long, trailing all the way to her hips. She looks beautiful, proud, and haughty, but the vision begins to fade away as drowsiness overwhelms me and I find myself drifting into a velvety comforting darkness.

Chapter 27

Gloom seems to have pervaded the very walls here of late, since a messenger issued recent despatches from France. Some of our men have fallen, not on the battlefield, but as a result of disease rampaging through the camp. It is difficult for us to imagine what life may be like in the field, but I hear supplies are low and that rain has plagued both progress and morale. Lady de Holmes, Matilda's cousin, who has been staying here with us, has recently been informed of her husband's death in battle. The news has overwhelmed her, and she has since confined herself to her chamber.

My new gown is delivered of me, serving to shine a little sunshine upon my melancholy. It is blue, the hue of the peacock and I am most glad of it. Henriette has despatched my other gown to the laundry and then it shall be trunked away until next spring.

I have taken Tenwyn's advice holding my head high, attending chapel dutifully and re-joining the ladies at work with the eternal needle and thread; even attending dance classes arranged by Lady Elowen. The weather has become colder, of late too wet to go riding, and pride has bid me to distance myself from William, even refusing to unseal the letters he has sent. Though I find my resolve is waning as melancholy is taking its grip, and Tenwyn's potion is having little effect.

It is cold even with the fire blazing. I bring my shawl tighter about my shoulders and rub my hands, for it is hard to work the tapestry with them so cold. I look at Kathryn sitting at the small window looking out and notice she is shivering. 'Pray Kathryn, join us, for you shall catch your death there,' I bid, since no one else seems troubled for her. She jumps, as though waking from a dream state, sighs, then capitulates to accompanying the rest of us around the fire.

Matilda looks around at us all, disdain on her face. 'Fetch the minstrels,' she snaps at a servant. 'I have had enough of the gloom here. You all feel sorry for yourselves, sitting here with a fire to warm your bellies, shelter over your heads and all that you need, whilst our men are fighting out in the cold, hungry and homesick. You are all faint hearted,' she rants. This sets off Kathryn, rising from her seat and rushing from the room in tears. I raise myself to go after her, but Matilda shouts me down. 'Oh, leave her,' she says. 'There are too many whimpering love-sick pups around here, misled by the masquerades of travelling players. What is wrong with women these days that they have no steel? It is no wonder that our men cannot wait to escape for the battlefield. Sentiment is a weakness. Should Henry manage to break the contract and forge a betrothal with the lady of his choice, then Kat will be at liberty to make a better match. Why do so many women allow their hearts to rule their heads? They are all just so weak!' I notice she is looking at me as she speaks.

'Pray madam, you are heartless,' I retort. 'We are all aware that Kathryn set her heart on Henry and her betrothal to him was set long ago. She feels betrayed, alas not by him alone, for his foul intentions have been common knowledge to all but her.'

'Oh, defend her as you will,' she snaps. 'I pray for the day when this wretched war is over, and we can all go on with our lives.'

I am vexed, no longer inclined to refrain from the burden I have been bearing upon my chest. 'Why did you send Father Arthur to my door?'

Matilda looks up from her embroidery. 'Lady Elizabeth, your husband contracted you into my care whilst he is away fighting the French. It has occurred to me that your health and disposition have been in decline and I deemed that some spiritual enrichment may assist you. I despatched my physician to you, though he has failed clearly, and I intend to have him replaced. The man is quite antiquated in his approach. It seems apparent that my endeavours are in vain since you are most ungracious.'

I refuse to listen to anymore, throwing my tapestry to the floor and leaving in haste, just as the minstrels arrive.

On reaching my chamber, I grab the top letter from William, and tear open its seal.

Dearest Beth

Whatever it is I have done to wound you, I pray beseech your forgiveness on bended knee. I miss our rides, the tree ... our tree and our beloved embrace.

William

I hurriedly write a letter, seal it and command Henriette to despatch it to William forthwith.

Chapter 28

I wake to the sound of the front door being opened and shake James, still in a deep sleep and groaning loudly in protest. 'Come on wake up, you're late,' I say glancing at the clock. Margot has arrived earlier than normal and the last thing I want is for her to discover us in bed together.

'Come on quickly, Margot's here already.'

'You got any painkillers, my head's killing me?'

I fetch some from the bathroom, then ruffle up the bedding in one of the spare rooms, to make it look as though he has been sleeping there. He is trying to pull his jeans on with one hand, with his phone in the other ringing work to make his excuses. I'm unable to stifle a laugh as he loses his balance and falls over.

James trails behind me as we bump into Margot on the stairs, still complaining about his sore head. 'Hi, Mason stayed over last night as he couldn't get a taxi. Would you mind sorting the spare bed for me?' I smile. She is po-faced as ever. 'Yes madam,' she says, frowning at James as they pass on the stairs.

I look at my watch in irritation. Rosa is ten minutes late and I wonder if she will even turn up. She has been avoiding me since my protests at the way she and James were brazenly flirting. She finally arrives out of breath. 'Sorry love, I couldn't get away,' she says removing her jacket.

'It's ok, I've got the drinks in.'

'God, do I need this after the morning I've had! She takes a large gulp of her gin and tonic. 'So, what's up?'

'Not a lot, I just thought it's been a while since we caught up and I was wondering why you haven't been answering my messages?'

'Well, Jimmy said you were pissed with me for some reason and I know you're going through a lot at the moment, so thought I'd give you some space.' Rosa looks at Eva serving behind the bar and waves to her. 'Poor darling, she was so excited about getting engaged, wasn't she? I nearly broke my neck last night tripping over that mutt of hers!' I realise she's trying to change the subject, so persevere doggedly.

'Well James and I are fine now,' I say in a firm voice. 'It was all a misunderstanding. As James said, you were quite drunk that night, and you can get touchy-feely when you're in that state. So, I apologise for doubting your loyalty as a friend.' I think my strategy has thrown her off balance, as she looks at me quizzically for a moment, but then throws a curveball right back at me.

'Oh Gracie, you do need some help dear. You are bound to be insecure with a husband like Lawrence. I don't want to patronize you, but I really think a course of counselling might be helpful.'

'No Rosa, there is nothing wrong with me and I do not need shit like that but thank you for your *friendly* advice. It's true that I have stuff to sort out, but I am more than capable of doing it on my own.' I look at my watch. 'Now I must go.' With no further ado, I leave, noting the surprised expression on her face.

Our brief discussion has done nothing but confirm my suspicions that she is no friend. Having taken Mason's advice about taking charge, my strength appears to be returning. I am finding his meditation techniques a great help, and in using the mirror as a focus, I no longer feel at the behest of my visions, having a much more positive approach to it all.

Chapter 29

'I knew you would be powerless to resist my charms for long,' William chuckles.

Rising from the blanket I smooth down my clothes and re-pin my hair as well as I am able. 'Sir, you have the guile of a warlock, yet word has it you are a rogue with a wandering lust, frequenting places best unspoken of.'

Helping with my cloak, he meets the challenge with a shrug of his shoulders and predictable nonchalance. 'Ah, you attend too much to washer-woman piffle-twaddle Beth.' Then, with no warning, he pushes me against the tree and meets my mouth with his own. I close my eyes and lose myself in the moment, all burdens and cares dissipating into the ether. When I open them, William's face has changed, not wholly, but his hair has altered and beard all but disappeared. No sooner than it arrived, the apparition is gone, yet my queer expression has startled him. 'Are you well Beth?' he asks with concern.

'Yes, quite fine, a little cold that is all. Let us ride back now.'

I am glad to find Tenwyn has responded to my behest, awaiting me in my chamber when I return from the ride.

Henriette approaches to assist with the removal of my cloak and riding boots. 'Why is the fire dying?' I demand. 'How dare you allow my guest to be cold in my chamber!' Insolent as ever, she does not respond. Shaking my head, I remove my gloves and rub my hands to warm them, bidding Tenwyn to take a seat.

'I have only just now arrived Beth,' he smiles kindly. 'How may I be of service?'

'I am quite sure nothing shall come of it, but I had a quarrel with Matilda this morning and she threatened your dismissal,' I explain.

'Dismiss me? Pray on what grounds?'

'I do not verily know sir. I believe she meant above all to wound me. Her accusation was false, that you are not assisting me as she bid you. I am affronted sir. Her aim is to injure me at every turn.'

'Pray be calm Beth, for all too often words are used as weapons.'

'And yet her enmity of me is boundless. What if she were to carry out her threat? What would you do and where would you go? Indeed, I know not what I should do without you here. Your soothing effect on my temper surpasses any potion.'

Tenwyn sits back in his chair contemplating, his fingers tousling with his beard. As I watch him his face alters, just as happened before with William, then reverts back.

'My lady?' he enquires, disarmed by my expression.

'Something queer is occurring Tenwyn. When I was with William earlier, his face changed, and for just a moment it was as if I was looking at somebody else. The same thing just occurred with you. Do you think I am bedevilled? Oh, good God, Matilda sent Father Arthur my way to restore my soul. What if they are both right? What am I to do?'

Henriette has brought wood to the fire and Tenwyn wisely remains silent whilst she stacks it carefully and all too leisurely. He signals caution to me. Again, I have been imprudent, my rash words spoken within earshot of an untrusty maid, failing to heed Tenwyn's advice. We wait patiently until she has completed her task, then I dismiss her. 'You need more reserve my lady,' he says simply.

'Yes, of this I am all too aware.' I look down at my hands folded in my lap and toy with my wedding band, feeling ashamed.

'I ask you to be circumspect for good reason, for words from the lips of a servant may spread like fire, becoming out of control and destructive. In these parts, poor folk recite tales of superstition to their children, and noblemen employ storytellers for amusement. People are taken from their homes on the hearsay of simple folk and tested as witches. Not that they would do that to you Beth, but if word were to reach your husband that you are deranged or bedevilled, he may admit you to a convent, or worse. Heed my warning, for castles are dangerous places.'

'I understand sir, but do you think I may be bedevilled, or deranged?'

'Neither. You are like me and my mother and grand-mother, endowed with the gift of seeing what others may not, and yet it carries many dangers.'

'But what of you being dismissed, if it were to occur? How would you seek to feed your family?'

'Then I should go on my travels seeking another position.' He looks at me fondly and I become overwhelmed with envy for his wife, for methinks Tenwyn is a rare gem within a trove of treasure.

Chapter 30

'I keep telling you Lawrence, we don't need her. I am not working and am quite happy to clean the house and make my own dinner.'

'Come on Grace, you don't have a clue how to keep a house, and you certainly can't cook. Frankly, I think you're ungrateful. You even refuse to get rid of a horse that you will never ride again. I give you a healthy allowance and you have the privilege of not having to work. I don't think you realise how lucky you are.'

'But Lawrence, I want to work. It's you who wants to keep me bound to the house.' There is a pause.

'Grace, you really don't get it do you? You really think you are hard done by. Anyway, enough said. Margot does a great job of maintaining the house and I like her. She stays.'

'Oh really? Well maybe you should divorce me and marry her instead!' I hang up on him for the first time in my life, surprising myself with the resurgence of long buried feistiness. Lawrence tries ringing again, but I ignore my mobile, and then the landline. I know he will be seething, but he can't lay a finger on me, because he is thousands of miles away. I am feeling stronger than ever, tired of being treated badly by everyone. I feel like a butterfly breaking free from a cocoon. I am learning to be more like the lady in blue.

When James rings me, I tell him I am planning a night in alone. I turn a blind eye to what Margot has prepared for my supper and cook a frozen pizza instead. Finally, I turn my phone off and turn on the television.

When I check my emails later, there is a message from Lawrence, entitled *Ungrateful Bitch*. I decide to put it on the back-burner, in no mood to read it right now. Nevertheless, as much as I try to forget about it, it remains in the back of my mind that I will have to read it eventually, like a black cloud bringing burden to a sunny day. I think of Mason and his calming influence. He would recommend I do some meditation.

I work through the exercises, relaxing my mind, and the mirror appears in my mind's eye spontaneously and unprompted. When I begin to focus on it, instantly my consciousness dives into a scene that could be straight from a film. The lady in blue is there as always. Across from her is the doctor figure, in whom I have seen Mason. They both appear silent, watching a servant laying wood on the fire. When she has finished and has left, they begin to speak and again I am left frustrated at not being able to hear anything. It is tantalizing, as though I am afforded only so much information, and it is then up to me to string everything together.

I am rudely drawn away from the scene by the trill of my mobile phone. I should never have turned the damned thing back on. In temper, I pick it up and throw it across the room and thankfully it lands on the sofa. Whoever invented these things has a lot to answer for.

Chapter 31

Preparing myself for the ride, I am interrupted by Father Arthur's entrance, and feel a nervous flush come over me at the sight of him. 'Father, to what do I owe you the honour? I am about to go riding. Is this a matter that may wait?'

Undeterred, he walks in boldly, clearly with no intention of leaving. 'This shall not take long my lady, just a few moments of your time.'

'Henriette, go bid Sir William to defer the ride.' She flurries away hurriedly, and Father Arthur takes a seat. I feel a chill run down my spine as he studies me earnestly with his small eyes. 'How have you fared since our last meeting my lady?'

'Unquestionably well Father.' I do my best to hide my unease as his small eyes view me with suspicion.

'Lady Elizabeth, my mission here is to protect the spiritual welfare of my brethren and it is not my desire to meddle, yet I heed you have not partaken in the sacramental confession of late?'

'Well, my incline is towards the old ways Father. I see no merit in wasting our gracious lord's time in the confession of mere trifles.'

His piercing gaze causes me to shift uncomfortably in my chair. 'You are mistaken Elizabeth, for it is clear that souls who choose to languish in the darkness shall receive no redemption, and their guilt may be signified by their renouncing of the confession.'

I find myself aghast at his words and notice my hands are beginning to shake. It has to be that witch Henriette who has brought this to my door, for I may think of no one else. I cast about for words that shall not further incriminate me. Laughing nervously, I conjure all the innocence I can muster. 'Pray, I know not your meaning Father.'

'As I cited, God has charged me with keeping my brethren's spirits chaste, unfettered from sin. It would seem that your physician's counsel may at times be inclined towards areas beyond his authority, instructing in the secret arts.'

I shake my head. 'Nay, Master Tenwyn is a beneficent gentleman, as should a physician be. He has proffered me potions to aid with my sleep and melancholy, that is all.'

Father Arthur fidgets in his chair.

'Pray, what advice did he offer for bedevilment, for I hear you have sought his counsel in these matters?'

Evidently under Matilda's command, Henriette has imparted our confidences to her, and in turn, she has apprised Father Arthur.

'Bedevilment Father? I see my maid has gravely misrepresented me. I was but speaking of my dreams to Master Tenwyn, nothing more, nothing less. She is but a meddling and unfaithful servant and I shall see to it that she is discharged upon my husband's return.'

Judging by his expression, he does not believe me. 'So, are you able to describe these dreams to me madam?'

'Oh, you know how dreams are, they come and go, and it is difficult to recollect them now. They were of no consequence I assure you, merely conveyed to Tenwyn as idle chat.'

'Perhaps we should probe your maid further if she has been lying as you would suggest?'

I find the courage to raise my voice a little. 'Trust me Father Arthur, that shall not be necessary. I am quite affronted that you should choose the words of a guttersnipe servant over the wife of a lord, sir.'

'Pray, forgive me for any offence my lady, but matters such as these are of extreme importance. Not only is it a danger for the person who may possessed, but for all those within reach of their company. Demons are verily masters of deception.'

My fear now has turned to anger, and I take a risk, rising to my feet holding my head high. 'Father, I shall hear no more of this nonsense. If it were true that I am bedevilled, I should rid this castle of most of those abiding within its walls, for their untrustworthiness and unfounded tittle-tattle! I am truly affronted sir and make no mistake that my husband shall hear of this.'

Father Arthur has lost a little of his self-righteousness, looking upon me with surreptitious uncertainty. Either my outburst shall have affirmed his suspicions that I am beyond doubt possessed, or he may have retracted at the threat of my husband's wrath. I wonder what other trifles Henriette may have conveyed, shivering at the thought.

'Think on it, madam. I am a servant of God, not your enemy. You have nothing to fear. Whether there is truth or not in this, be not succumbed to deception. We each of us have a duty in being God's true servants.' He rises and makes his way to the door and I compose myself quickly to compensate for having been overly-bold.

'I thank you Father. Pray forgive me my indiscretions. I have merely been in disbelief at the accusations thrown at my door.' I cross myself as he leaves, then find my entire body tensing, clenching my fists angrily.

Henriette has been gone a long time and I doubt not she shall be fearing her return. She has just cause to do so.

Chapter 32

I watch Mason meticulously placing tobacco in a rolling paper. 'Have you been finding the meditation helpful?' he asks.

'Yes, I still struggle a bit clearing my mind, but now that I've begun practising every day, I feel it is helping a lot. The mirror works well, sometimes I only have to think about it and I'm already there, straight in. I've taken your advice and am writing everything down, beginning to piece things together a little at a time. It feels like I'm spying in on another world and I'm actually enjoying it now. By the way, I've have decided to give my lady a name. My middle name is Elizabeth, so I'm going to call her that from now on.'

'Sounds like a good plan. So, has there been anything of interest lately?'

'Well, in my vision last night she had a priest with her. He seemed quite intimidating like he was chastising her, and she looked nervous. Why would anyone be afraid of a priest?'

'Well, the church was good at inciting fear back then.'

'It reminds me of the phrase, *the fear of God*. It doesn't make any sense that God would want his followers to be scared of him. I was brought up by my grandparents who were Catholics and had to go to church regularly until I was a teenager. Religion never really resonated with me, even as a child. I do believe in God though. How could I not after my NDE? It's hard to put into words, but I felt an overwhelming sense of peace and love in the afterlife that could never really be experienced here. To me, God is an omnipotent force that is all-seeing, all-knowing and all-loving.'

Now that Mason has finished preparing his roll-up, we venture outside to smoke on the patio. The weather is overcast and a little chilly, so I go back for my coat. 'I'm going to have to quit these soon, before Lawrence gets back,' I say as I light up. Right on cue, I hear my mobile ringing and I know it will be him. Swearing, I stub out my cigarette and go back inside to answer. We haven't spoken since I hung up on him yesterday. He asks if I have read his e-mail. 'No, I've been too busy,' I say. 'Look, I'm sorry about my rant. It's not just about having Margot around, but as I'm not working, I feel I should at least be contributing in the house.'

'Are you sure you haven't got anything to hide? Is that the real reason you don't want Margot there?'

'No, of course not.'

'Well Margot is staying, ok? I will accept your apology, but I'm tired of your selfish attitude Grace. I'm the one working for a living, here in a god-forsaken country, not knowing what you're up to half the time. You ignore your phone and are so damn secretive.' By now, I am holding the mobile away from my ear as his pitch has steadily increased. Through the patio doors I watch Mason shaking his head, smiling at me, as I roll my eyes. Lawrence pauses, waiting for a response, but I give none. 'Are you there?'

'Yes Lawrence, I have apologised, and you've said your piece. Now, can we move on please?' He hangs up and I go back outside.

'Why does he always make me feel like shit?' I ask Mason, lighting up again. 'I mean, he has a knack of twisting things to make everything my fault. It's doing my head in.'

'Because he's clever Grace and you've got to learn to meet him. Look, it's really none of my business, but every time he phones when I'm around, he always seems to be having a go at you. Yes, he's got money and you've got a great home, but is it worth all this grief?' He looks down at his feet considering whether or not to go on. 'Tell me if I'm speaking out of turn, but Rosa told me hit you?'

Rosa and her big mouth! I inhale on my cigarette deeply as if it's my life-saver. This is a place I choose not to venture at the moment. 'Well, it's complicated,' I say defensively. 'We have a lot of stuff to sort out when he gets back. Mind you I do have to try and see things from his point of view, that he has a stressful job and it can't be easy being so far from home. The main problem is his drinking, but he won't admit it.'

'We all have our issues, Grace. But you don't treat someone consistently badly if you really love them. You certainly know how to pick them, what with him and Dickhead!'

I laugh. 'Oh, I take it you mean James? What about you Mason, you're a great looking guy. I'm surprised you haven't got a girlfriend.'

'I prefer to be on my own right now. I was in a serious relationship for five years. We were engaged, but she did the dirty on me.'

'I'm sorry to hear that.'

'It was painful at the time, but it just wasn't meant to be. I'm over it now, but one thing I learnt is that life is too short to mess around. I always knew it wasn't going to work, in my gut, but stuck with it doggedly. Look, I know I haven't known you very long Grace, but I care about you. I don't know your husband, but it sounds like he's taking out his own issues on you, rather than taking responsibility for them. He doesn't deserve you and you're on a slippery slope if he's abusing you. Then there's James, who is shallow, just a good-time boy. I'm sorry love but I have to say it as I see it. Don't you think it's time to wake up and smell the coffee?'

His words sting and all at once I feel weighed down with guilt, hurt and embarrassment. 'Well, you sure know how to make a woman feel good,' I remark. But I know in my heart he is right. As hard as I try, I can't hold back the tears, suddenly feeling vulnerable like a lost child. 'I'm a bloody mess, aren't I?' I say, wiping away smudged mascara from around my eyes.

Mason stubs out his cigarette and holds out his long arms for me to sink into, gently patting my back. 'I'm sorry Grace, I hate upsetting you, I'm just trying to help.'

I look up at him. 'You are a true friend, the only one I feel I have. You know you'd make a good counsellor. You always seem to say the right thing at the right time. But there again you were a doctor in that other life, so I'm not all that surprised. Thank you, Mason.'

Chapter 33

The coward stayed away all night, now sneaking in mid-morning in the hope that I may be absent out riding, but she has misjudged me, for I have been in my chamber hotly awaiting her return. And as she arrives, I fast approach her, taking her unawares, slapping her haughty face hard, causing her to lose her balance, nearly falling from the impact. 'I always knew you to be an unfaithful servant,' I cry. 'You are not worthy of occupation and I shall see to it that you return to poverty and misery. How dare you forsake me, prattling malignant gossip and untruths. If I had my way I would bolt you to the stocks and leave you there until you rot!'

She is in shock, nursing her cheek with her right hand. 'I know not of what you speak,' she says insolently.

'Is that so? Then why have you kept away all this time since my audience with Father Arthur? I shall cast you aside, for you are treacherous, brazen and idle.'

Now I march from my chamber to the solar, finding the ladies excitedly skimming through an array of colourful fabrics for new gowns. Matilda, in audience with the seamstress, looks up in surprise at my unexpected visit. 'Elizabeth...'

'I need a new servant at once!' I proclaim breathlessly. 'My maid is ill-equipped and disloyal.'

The ladies look at one another in surprise and Matilda raises her head haughtily. 'It is not my remit to replace a servant under the employ of your husband and neither shall I become involved in your domestics. This is a matter for Edward, not me.'

'He is not here Matilda and I cannot abide her presence a moment longer. Does she spy for you, or Father Arthur?'

'My dear Elizabeth, many of us are, and have been, troubled about your well-being.'

'That, Matilda, is an ill-adorned jest. I vow my well-being is not incumbent upon visitations from your chaplain. I beseech you, who has the maid been spying for?'

Matilda turns her back on me quipping 'you are deluded madam' under her breath.

'Very well, I shall write to my husband, bidding her dismissal.' Turning on my heel and gathering my skirts, I leave hurriedly. In truth I shall not write to him, for I know he shall not want domestic issues that he would deem as trifling, brought to his door. Furthermore, I do not wish him prying into the frightful undertakings here, for he is pre-disposed to wrath over understanding. I shall have to keep the maid for now, though she shall not find me a kind mistress, nor shall she ever be present again in the company of my guests.

I march back to my chamber to find Henriette nursing her face with a damp cloth. I tut, 'you prissy, it was but a slap and far less than you deserve. Take it as a warning that if you should EVER forsake me again, I shall cast you straight back to your village hovel. Now, fetch me my physician.' She looks at me sullenly, then bolts out the door.

When Tenwyn arrives, I assign Henriette to errands in town. He listens attentively, stroking his beard, as I explain everything to him. 'My lady,' he says, 'you are apt to court drama. Pray heed caution, for it is unwise to cross a priest, and you have but few allies. I beg you cease seeing Sir William for it is too dangerous. Forgive me, but he is a fiend and a rogue, and your dalliance is reckless. I do not wish to see you get hurt.'

'Oh Tenwyn, I am so tired of it all here. I know I am doltish, yet William is a beacon in this dark castle. I have tried to cast him aside, but without him, there is nothing here for me; nothing! And yes, I am rash and foolhardy, for I was born with fire in my belly. I am lacking in tact and judgement, yet I cannot change my nature.' I look fondly at Tenwyn and he smiles. 'Aye, and you were born with the mind of a mule,' he says.

'Whilst you sir, are a veritable angel amongst a pack of wolves,' I respond.

Chapter 34

The haze in the mirror clears to reveal Elizabeth's maid entering her room. She is waif-like but has a shiftiness about her. In fact, she resembles Margot a little, albeit a younger version. Elizabeth appears to have been waiting for her and looks angry. I watch as she strides towards the girl and slaps her face, causing her to lose balance. Then she shouts at her and rushes from the room, leaving the girl in shock, nursing her cheek.

The image fades, and once again I am left frustrated to glean only a part of the story, wondering what her maid had done to upset Elizabeth. As ever, I am a witness only, there being no sound in these visions. Today, I am transporting Caesar to his new abode at the riding stables, but first, I should document what I saw in the mirror.

Caesar and I are very close, having an almost telepathic relationship. I can't help but feel guilty for not having ridden him since the accident and am taking him to the riding school for his own benefit, as well as to appease Lawrence. I know though that he will find it dreary taking young children on short trips, when his real passion is like my own, tearing through the countryside. For me there is no feeling like it. The rush and exhilaration is like a drug pumping through my veins, a raw abandonment, leaving behind all worldly cares. I love a quote I once heard: *The horse and rider shall be one beast*. For both our sakes, I am determined to find a way some day to combat my fear and get back in the saddle.

Caesar's initial apprehension of his new surroundings has been ameliorated by the whiff of fellow horses. I pat his shoulder, as he munches on a carrot with one eye on me, as I speak to him. 'I am not leaving you boy. I shall come each day to feed you and muck you out. You'll make a lot of friends here and the children will love you as you help them to learn to ride. And when I am fit enough, we will go for long rides together again, I promise you.' Even though he appears to be settled, I can't help but feel I'm letting him down as I drive away.

When I arrive home, I check my emails, reluctantly opening Lawrence's one that is entitled *Ungrateful Bitch*. It starts off with the usual rant about how selfish my behaviour is and then he mentions something which sends a shiver all the way down my spine. *Even Margot thinks you have been behaving strangely.* Margot? What could he mean? Why would he have spoken to her? I wait for her to arrive back after her lunch break, approaching her as soon as she enters the hallway. She looks surprised to see me. 'Oh, hello madam,' she says. As ever, I find her form of address an irritation.

'When did you last speak to my husband?' I ask.

'Oh, um, a few days ago when he rang to speak to you. He said he couldn't get hold of you on your mobile, so he rang the landline and you weren't here, so I answered.'

'And what did you say?' Margot appears a little awkward. 'Well, I told him you weren't at home.'

'Just that Margot? Something else must have been said because he told me he spoke to you.' She is shaking her head. I always knew I couldn't trust her. She removes her coat, placing it on the peg and switches her shoes for the pumps she wears about the house. 'I can't say I recall anything else madam,' she states nonchalantly.

I know she is lying. 'Well in future if the phone rings, please do not answer it. I shall change the set up on the answer-machine.'

I wonder if Lawrence's getting her to spy on me now that I've said I don't want her here. What does she know? I think of all the secrets I am holding from him. I dismiss her early, as I can't bear her presence in the house, especially if she is spying on me. I shall have to be more cautious in future. Spotting my diary on the coffee table where I have been documenting my visions, I wonder if she has been reading it. I recollect the vision I had just this morning, where Elizabeth was angry with her maid.

Coincidence?

Chapter 35

Save for the crackling of fire embers, all is deathly quiet, and the castle's pervasive gloom enshrouds me. Henriette is playing truant, shirking from her duties. The pot has not been emptied, neither has she replenished the water for my wash. The rushes are as yet unchanged and there is very little firewood remaining. I decide I shall write to Edward after-all, since the girl's in-subordinance is quite beyond the bounds of acceptability. As I pick up my quill, there is a knock at the door. Since I have no servant, I am obliged to call forth whomever it is. I feel of flush of anticipation that it may be William, whom I have not seen for two days. Alas, it is not, for it is Father Arthur, shadowed by a lady of the convent. They appear quite the comedy; he being short and portly, the cord at his waist barely able to contain his belly, whilst she is tall and very slender.

'Father.' I cross myself, wondering what mischief he brings to my door this time. I had hoped that my frankness at our last meeting may have deterred him from another visitation. 'Pray be seated,' I say, wondering how I am to accommodate my guests with no servant and a dying fire. This is most awkward, and the wench shall pay gravely. 'I am afraid my servant is about her errands Father. May I offer you both mead?'

'Nay thank you,' he responds on both their behalves. 'This is Sister Frances from the Priory of Saint Margaret.' She is

bedecked in a coarse, off-white wool habit, with an imposing wooden cross hanging low from her neck. Her wimple frames a long stern face and frosty countenance.

'I am aware of what happened to the girl,' Father Arthur remarks blankly. The little guttersnipe must have gone running to Matilda, proffering yet more ammunition for her venomous campaign.

I raise my head haughtily. 'My upbringing Father has taught me to distrust unruly servants. The girl is quite unsuited to serve. She has neither prowess nor obedience.'

'Nevertheless, striking a servant is improper madam and your actions have ratified my suspicions, that dark forces are indeed working through you. Your soul is devoid of sanctity and requires purging, for you are a peril not just unto yourself, but to us all here. Sister Margaret shall be pleased to accompany you for a brief sojourn at the priory. I am confident that the environment and the work of women in a holy place shall be your saviour.'

I rise to my feet. 'You astonish me sir. How dare you speak to me so! That you shall listen to the imaginings and falsehoods my enemies have brought to your door. There is nothing amiss with me, save this castle, which IS full of demons and not just hidden ones.'

Sister Frances crosses herself nervously and Father Arthur rises to his feet. 'My duty is to protect my Lord and Lady de Bray and all those who abide under their roof. If you shall not see reason, then I am duty-bound to appeal to your husband.' They leave without further ado.

I sink to my knees in utter despair.

Chapter 36

Fresh from a shower, I make my way into the living room rolling my hair into the turban, to find James sitting with his feet on the coffee table, watching television. I am beginning to regret having given him a spare key, because he seems to be taking too much for granted.

'Well, hello there, stranger. I thought you'd forgotten about me,' I say, thinking how unsightly I must look in my dressing gown and turban on my head.

He smiles, 'I've been working late, as Keith's off, and I've had to deal with his clients.'

'Well, I understand all that, but you might have called me,' I say curtly.

'Yeah, you're right, sorry. Are you ok with me staying here tonight as my room-mates are having friends over?'

'As long as you leave early before Margot turns up. We could watch a film perhaps?' We are interrupted by his phone, which I take as an opportunity to tidy myself in the bathroom. James shouts out to me. 'There's a party tonight, it's Adam's birthday.'

'Oh, are we are both invited? Who told you about it?'

'Rosa.'

But of course. She hasn't bothered to contact me but has invited James along. 'I'm not sure I want to go James, not if Rosa's going to be there,' I say, rubbing my hair with the towel. But that would just play into her hands, so perhaps I should go with James, showing a united front, just to piss on her fireworks.

'It's up to you, but I'm going anyway,' he says casually, which helps me decide. 'Great, I'll go and get ready,' I say chirpily.

I wear my new peacock blue silk dress and high heels, making a special effort, out to make a statement, mainly for Rosa's benefit. As we walk in the village hall hand in hand, I take a deep breath and hold my head up high. When Rosa spots us, she looks surprised, no doubt disappointed that I have turned up with James. She carries on chatting to the small group she is with, making no effort to come to greet us. She too has dressed for impact, wearing a short emerald green dress and ridiculously high black heels, showing off her long legs. The village hall is packed and the music suitably loud with red lights dancing on all the walls. I make my way over to a couple of people I know, Sophia and Helen, feeling a little uncomfortable being here without an official invite. I know Adam, but only as an acquaintance, another of Rosa's friends who she has slept with. Sophia puts my mind at rest by saying that he invited all those who regularly frequent the Laughing Pig.

The three of us go to dance and I soon find my rhythm, enjoying myself more than I have done in ages. After a-while, the track changes to a song I don't like very much, and I look around for James, spotting him at the bar laughing and joking with Rosa. I carry on dancing, then when I next look, I see Rosa reaching up to say something in his ear and James laughing raucously. Then, I notice his hand lightly touching her bottom. Leaving the dance floor, I stride over to the bar furiously. Rosa smiles at me falsely and James appears awkward. I ask him to get me a drink and Rosa skulks off like a surly cat, swaying her hips as she goes, conceitedly looking around for admirers, for new prey to flirt with, and I find myself wondering how I ever could have valued her as a friend.

I invite James outside for a cigarette and, feeling brave from the alcohol, I ask him directly if he has been seeing Rosa.

He exhales a puff of smoke, looking at me intently. 'She's right,' he says. 'You are paranoid.'

'Who said I'm paranoid?'

'Rosa.'

'Oh of course, she would say that wouldn't she?' I say with heavy sarcasm.

'Well, you have been acting weird lately, all these bloody visions and stuff. Rosa says you need counselling and I think she's right.'

'Oh, she does, does she? Well, it seems like you hang on her every word. You know what, you are welcome to each other!' I shout. I storm off towards the road, then remember to go back for my jacket. James doesn't react, just stands there puffing on his cigarette. On the way to the cloakroom, I pass Rosa, shoving her out the way rudely, nearly sending her flying. I rush past before she can say anything, grab my jacket and start to make my way home, a mile, and a half in these damned heels! I find myself shivering in my thin jacket as rain begins to fall from the sky. I know I am vulnerable dressed like this, walking through town alone late at night, but I really don't care.

Angry tears stream down my face. It is over. James and I are finished.

Chapter 37

Ever looking for an excuse to throw a banquet, Matilda has arranged a celebration in honour of her cousin's wife Elena, who has recently borne her first healthy son, to advance the family line. Sadly, Elena herself is unable to attend as she is still abed in considerable pain, whilst her son abides in the nursery with his wet-nurse. Her husband is in France, though word shall no doubt reach him 'ere long. The great hall is heaving, and I always find it remarkable that such a cold barren room with silent walls may become so transformed into an array of colour and verve. Again, Matilda has invited kinsmen from all about, with as many men as possible to counter the balance of ladies, despite the majority being in their senior years. The music is drowned out by the sound of chat and laughter. For once my fingers and toes are not numb with cold. Even the hearty fires and tapestries covering the walls are not usually enough to fend off the damp and cold at this time of the year, other than on occasions such as this.

I am in no mood for revelry, yet it is a distraction from the turmoil that I find myself in, uplifted a little by my new gown of silk of a hue to match the peacock's feather, a material I had difficulty resisting at the merchant's last visit.

This affair is less formal than the last and I am glad to be seated with strangers on either side of me. A fanfare proclaims the arrival of Matilda, also adorned in a new gown, of emerald green with gold embroidery, and I muse at how well her bedazzling appearance seems to veil an inherent streak of malevolence. She loftily takes her place in her grand chair at the centre of the dais, assuming the authority of a queen courted by her subjects. Isabella, her only child, takes her place beside her. She is slender like her mother, though unfortunately resembles her father in countenance, with a disposition unduly solemn for a girl so young. Matilda complains often that children are hard to come by with an ever-absent husband, forever drafted away by the king to do his bidding.

I look up in surprise to see William come up behind Isabella and taking his place on the other side of Matilda, evidently as her guest of honour. Whatever may this mean? Is this why he has kept from me these past days, telling me he had important duties to attend to? What an effrontery that my lover may be cossetted with my greatest adversary, a woman would condemn me to a convent for the rest of my days!

The steward hammers on the table to quieten us all, that Matilda may speak. She rises to her feet and I watch William looking up at her admiringly. So vexed am I that I pay no attention to her speech. Verily I should like to slap the priggish expression from William's face as he looks about the room, seeking admiration from the ladies. Like a docile pony I fell for his charm, his wit, and handsome looks, trusting in his affection and admiration. Yet he is a false cuckold, treating me as he would a harlot from a tavern. I have given of myself wilfully, bargaining both reputation and marriage, in trust of true sentiment over dalliance. What kind of a dolt am I?

My ire propels me to a state of stillness, so that when I look about the room, all appears as though nothing is real. I look back at William, and for a moment his face shifts, in the way that it has done so before. It is as though he may read my mind, for he looks my way and we lock eyes and once again it is William's face that I see. I throw him a look of displeasure and he looks away ungraciously.

Finally, the food is brought forth, delivered first to the top table, tray after tray. There is roast swan, boars head, salted fish, and a myriad of delicacies, yet I have no appetite for neither food nor jollity. Indeed, the sight of it all makes me feel nauseas. Our goblets are filled with the finest wine from the cellars. The lady to my right introduces herself, bringing me back to my senses. As we speak, I notice Matilda slyly looking my way, and I return to her a look of distain.

I eat very little and when the plates are cleared from the tables, a jester brings merriment and laughter to all it seems but me. I find more interest in watching Matilda and William and the way in which they gaze at one another as they laugh at the jester's antics. And the casual touch to the arm does not go unnoticed.

It is when they go to lead the dance that I find it all determinedly too much to bear, retreating forthwith to my chamber.

Chapter 38

I'm not so keen on the Drunken Duck pub as it is smaller and has less atmosphere than the Laughing Pig, but Rosa often goes there in her lunch break and she is the last person I want to see right now.

'So how are things now that you've finally seen the light and dumped James?' Mason asks, wiping beer froth away from under his nose.

'Well, I've cleared all his stuff out of the house, all neatly thrown in the bin. I'd be lying to say I am leaping up and down with joy, but I guess I am well rid. I really thought he had feelings for me.'

'You'd be surprised at the lengths some blokes go to get a girl into bed Grace. I told you, he's just a good-time boy.'

'I guess the rose-tinted spectacles are off now. To begin with I looked on him as my knight in shining armour, but I suppose I've always known in my heart he wasn't right for me.'

Mason looks at me intently. 'So, if you're happily married, what exactly are you looking to be saved from?'

I laugh. 'You have a way of shooting the arrow right at the target, don't you Mason? It's true that I am one to bury my head in the sand. My relationship with Lawrence was great until we got married.'

'What happened then?'

'Well, I suppose we had a few problems, like everyone does. Lawrence has always been a drinker, but he seemed to get worse when he was made redundant and I know he doesn't like working abroad, but it's a good job and the money's great. We've been trying to start a family and that's caused a lot of strain. Lawrence is desperate for a child and holds it against me that I can't get pregnant.'

'It's not your fault.'

'I know, but if he can't have his way, he is apt to become aggressive.'

'So where do you see things now?'

'Well, I'm toughening up. I'm so fed up with people treating me badly; Lawrence, then Rosa, now James. I've begun to stand my ground more with Lawrence and he hates it. It's strange but Elizabeth is very feisty, and I feel she is rubbing off on me. Do you think that's possible?'

Mason looks thoughtful. 'It's hard to say as some people change naturally when they are pushed too far. I suppose it is possible that you are merging with her consciousness. No doubt you are influencing each other.'

'Maybe. I just find it mind-blowing that we might be sharing the same soul and that I could be her future self, watching her.'

Our sandwiches arrive and Mason shifts in his chair, waiting for the waitress to leave. 'Yes, I think it's probably rare for someone to experience over-lapping lifetimes like you are doing, but there again it's not unusual for people who have had NDE's to report curious psychic experiences. Just because things aren't accepted by society, doesn't mean they don't exist. We accept electricity, even though it is invisible. It is my belief that we are multi-dimensional beings experiencing many levels of being simultaneously. In your case, I find it hard to believe it is all purely random. There must be some message or a lesson to learn from it, so it's important to pay attention.'

'Yes, I'm trying to piece it all together. I find it odd that I am able to recognise people I know in that other lifetime. Not just that, but there seem to be a lot of over-lapping events. Like yesterday, I saw some sort of a feast going on at the castle. Elizabeth's lover was sitting next to the castle's mistress and they both seemed to be flirting. Elizabeth looked upset by this and the entire scene reminded me of Adam's party the other night, when Rosa and James both humiliated me with their outrageous behaviour.' The memory of that night still riles me, and I have to take a deep breath to calm myself down.

'So, are you suggesting that Rosa is the castle's mistress and James is Elizabeth's lover and that things occurring there are on a parallel with the present day?'

'Yes, exactly!'

Mason nods smiling, his pale blue eyes meaningfully meeting with mine. 'That's pretty interesting. So are you sure that the man you are referring to, aka James, is Elizabeth's lover and not her husband?'

'Without a doubt. They are very secretive, and I know she's married because she wears a huge wedding ring. It's odd though because there don't seem to be a lot of men around the castle.'

'That's probably because they were away fighting. Men could spend years away from home in those times. Perhaps the castle is a kind of a refuge for the ladies. I wonder if Elizabeth's husband is away like yours, and she too has been playing away with an arsehole?'

I laugh. 'Well, it's certainly food for thought.'

'Right, I've got to get back,' Mason says reaching for his jacket. 'Keep recording it all and we'll speak again soon.'

'Thanks Mason, if it weren't for you, I'd probably be a neurotic zombie by now, pumped full of tranquilizers.'

When I arrive back home, the place is a mess, but I am happy because Margot isn't here. She's had to travel back to France to care for her sick mother, or so she tells me. I can't help but wonder if it has anything to do with me chastising her for speaking to Lawrence, as she has appeared quite surly since then. Whatever the reason, I am glad, for once not feeling like a prisoner in my own home.

It must be night-time as the room is dimly-lit. Then I see Elizabeth sitting up in bed, tousles of hair hanging loose from her night bonnet. She's staring into space and looks so sad and alone. If only I could detect what she is thinking. Is she upset about her lover betraying her, like James has me? I certainly know how painful that is. I just wish I could bring her some comfort. I imagine myself moving to the side of the bed and placing my hand gently on her head. She suddenly starts and leaps out of her bed, making me jump straight back to the room.

She felt it. She felt me touching her!

Chapter 39

The view from the turret is splendid. As a means of distraction from despair and ennui, I have become accustomed to climbing the steep winding staircase right to the top each day. On the southern horizon lies the coast, and on a clear day, I am just able to view the glimmering green ocean. The north is where I usually ride, a craggy bleak landscape crowned by lush forests in the distance. I draw my cloak tight against the harsh cold wind and rub my hands together, still numb despite wearing gloves. Children are playing Chase the Fox in the courtyard down below. Their innocence and zest shall be drawn from them as they grow into adulthood with all of its burdens, I muse.

William has kept from me, fortuitous for him, for I assuredly would proffer him no dainty reception. Yesterday I went riding alone, despite Master Hedyn's babble. Now that William has forsaken me, the ride is my only joy. Kathryn has attested that he spends his nights in the solar with Matilda, playing cards or chess. He has laid bare his colours, humiliating, and leaving me bereft.

I wonder when my husband shall return. There have been rumours of a monstrous ambush bringing casualties amongst our men. Edward has not written for some time and I have no news that may bring him cheer. I am informed that the ague ensues in Suffolk and has rampaged as far as London.

Henriette went running to Matilda, refusing to serve me further. For her sake it is just as well, for I would have maimed the little rat 'ere long. She is now in the employ of Lady Butterford and I have her maid Mary, a quiet girl who is more dutiful, though I may not trust her either, since she will have been charged by Matilda or fat Arthur to watch me as a hawk may survey its prey. I have been attending mass like a devout choir girl each day, watching my steps carefully, ever aware of small eyes looking for signs of hysteria or possession. I live in dread of Arthur's threat to write to Edward that I am toying with demons, and that my only hope of redemption is a confinement within the walls of the sisterhood. Lord forgive me, but I can think of nothing more harrowing than such a predicament.

I have committed the sin of adultery and my soul is damned, as I may not trust the clergy here to make the confession. Such an act would be tantamount to signing my death warrant since Father Arthur 'ere seeks more fuel to add to his fire. Therefore, I have submitted a summons to my own priest back in Gippeswic, in the hope that he has not himself been afflicted by the ague. Father Michael is a man I may trust, a true man of the cloth, whereas to me, it appears that fat Arthur is enshrouded by an unholy darkness. I cross myself quickly as I recall the words of my childhood tutor, to be forever deferential for a man of the cloth, for he has been anointed as God's divine messenger. I was chastised as an errant child, yet it was in vain, for I have not altered.

I have but few cherished memories to recall from my childhood, yet my joy was boundless, when on my fifth birthday, I was presented with my first palfrey. I named her Daisy after my favourite flower, as she brightened my days, affording me freedom away from the nursery. I was a quick *learner and riding very soon became my passion. Eventually I was permitted to venture further afield out into the countryside, to lush forests and beautiful meadows that filled the senses with colour and aroma, the sun beaming down on me and a fresh breeze flushing my cheeks. Ah, that I could go back to those times of innocence. Riding was, and still is, my heaven. I recall weeping wretchedly when the winter set in, for I was forbidden to ride again until the following spring.*

My contemplation is disturbed by the sound of footsteps, someone hurriedly climbing the steep winding steps. It is Mary, flushed and breathless from the exertion. 'My lady, you have a visitor,' she says holding onto her chest.

I make my way back down the steps and into my chamber. A lady has her back to me, warming her hands by my lively fire.

It is Matilda.

Chapter 40

Driving back from the stables, I am more relaxed now that Caesar appears to be adapting well to his new surroundings. I was heartened to be greeted by him twitching his ears, a sure sign of him being pleased to see me. I think back to my fifth birthday when my grandparents surprised me with a pony, *Joey*. He was a gift from heaven, fulfilling a dream I had had for as long as I could remember. I was raised by my grandparents from the age of six months, as my mother was a drug addict and unable to cope. I have never known my father, or even who he is. When I turned sixteen, my mother decided she wanted to see me, even though she had never before tried to make contact, not even as much as sending me birthday cards. Neither had she been in touch with my grandparents all those years. On the one hand I was curious to meet her, but that alone was not enough, so I declined. It is not just me she let down, but my grandparents, which I find frankly unforgiveable.

Sadly, my grandparents are no longer here, and I often feel alone in the world. My upbringing was somewhat sheltered, but they supported me always and I realise only now how fortunate I was and how things could have worked out so differently. I miss them both so much, especially my grandmother who passed just last year from a second heart attack.

As I pull into the driveway, I break from my reminiscing, noticing a blue Audi parked there and Rosa is standing at my front door.

As I shut the car door, she greets me with an insincere smile, moving to one side as I approach the front door.

'What do you want Rosa?' I ask coldly.

'I was passing, and thought I'd pop in to see how you are. I haven't seen you in ages.' She rudely enters the house removing her coat, even though I haven't invited her in.

'But you haven't been answering my calls or texts Rosa.' I stride into the living room and watch as she awkwardly perches herself on the edge of the sofa, whilst I stand there with my hands on my hips.

'Look, I know things haven't been exactly right between us lately, for all sorts of reasons, but...'

'Yes, like poaching my boyfriend,' I interrupt cynically.

'Oh, come on Grace, you were never serious about James. You said yourself it would never work. It was merely a fling while hubby's away.'

I feel my face flush with anger. 'I don't know what *Jimmy* has been telling you, but I'm not like you, not the type to sleep around.'

'For God's sake Grace, stop deluding yourself. That's exactly what you did, sleep with another man behind your husband's back. I'm not married, I'm a free agent.'

'Free to stab your friend in the back Rosa, yes that's what you did. But if you can live with yourself, then carry on. It's not the first time you've broken up a relationship. But worse than that, you do it and then move on to the next unwitting prey. Oh yes, I've seen it loads of times. You have things to face up to as well. You can't go around messing up peoples' lives just because you are single.'

Rosa is now in a rage herself and makes for the door. 'Fine,' she says turning on her heel. 'I came here to offer an olive branch, but it's been a complete waste of time.'

'No Rosa, you came here to appease your own conscience. You and James are welcome to each other. Now please leave my property.' I usher her to the door and slam it shut behind her. Then I notice she has left her coat behind, so open the door and throw it, watching it land on the wet paving. She shouts after me as she opens her car door. 'Well I hope hubby doesn't find out, 'cos it'll mean another beating,' is her parting shot.

Chapter 41

Matilda turns away from the fire, greeting me with a false smile. 'Elizabeth dear, since we have not had the grace of your company in the solar, I wondered if you were unwell? I have been apprised of a noteworthy physician who may be of service to you, for I am most disenchanted with Master Tenwyn.'

'I am quite well madam. I have no need of physicians, priests, or the sanctuary of a nunnery. My disquiet has nothing to do with my body or spirit. It is merely that I miss my own friends, my home, my lands, my... my life. Here; and please do not bid me ungracious, but here there is nothing for me.' It pains me that I may not protest that she has pilfered William from my bosom to her own. Adultery is a lonesome sin, a deep dark secret best kept in an empty silent room.

Matilda stares under hooded dark eyes with a coldness that sends a chill down my back. 'I am aware that the cold weather has hindered your pleasure of the ride, therefore it is prudent is it not that you share the great company of our ladies here? For you are not the only one here who is away from their homely comforts and we are all called to endure without our husbands. As your guardian and host I am accountable for your welfare and brooding in your chamber just shall not do. You must be more robust, Elizabeth. I shall send my new physician to you, for it is clear that Tenwyn has done little to improve your condition.'

I am aghast. 'Pray madam, how so that you deem my discontent in residing here be termed as a condition? What potion would you profess for treating such Matilda?' I shake my head rigorously. 'Nay, I shall not see your new physician. Master Tenwyn has assisted me in ways where no one else is able, and it is he whom I shall accommodate when I should deem it necessary.'

'Oh, so what does he carry in his bag that helps you my dear? What potions does he proffer? I am told that he uses the old craft, the ways of his ancestors who were witches. He should heed caution and so should you Elizabeth. Who knows what mischief he may have brought to your door?' She glares at me with the charm of a snake, then picks up her skirts and strides from my chamber.

I glance at Mary standing in the corner, shock on her face. 'Mary, fetch me Master Tenwyn forthwith,' I command.

Chapter 42

I reach to my bedside table for my notepad and pen to document what I have just witnessed in the mirror. Elizabeth appeared to be having another confrontation with the castle's mistress and, as I write, I think back to the altercation I had with Rosa yesterday. Is this another coincidence?

I'm feeling a little shabby this morning, finding it hard to concentrate and wonder if I am going down with a cold. As I reach up to the medicine cabinet for the painkillers, I am suddenly overcome by queasiness and dash to the bathroom, getting there just in time to vomit in the toilet. Going through all that I ate yesterday, I can't think of anything that may have given me a bad stomach. I phone the stables to let them know I won't be turning up today, feeling a little guilty because they have come to rely on me helping out on a voluntary basis, they being short-staffed at the moment. I am grateful to them for taking on Caesar and as I visit him each day, I am only too pleased to help out. Today though, I have very little energy, so resign myself to taking it easy. In all, I vomit four times and can eat nothing. I can't even face drinking coffee.

I feel a little better by the afternoon, so set myself the task of cleaning up the house.

The following morning, I wake in a cold sweat from my recurring horse-chase nightmare. There was one small difference this time in that, in the dream, I was Elizabeth, not

Grace. I never get to see what happens next, waking either during the flight or from a sense of falling. Before I get to document my dream, I have to dash to the bathroom for another vomiting episode. When I get back to the bedroom there is a message on my phone from Mason asking how I am. It never ceases to amaze me how he seems to have a sixth sense of when I am struggling with something.

He calls again that evening, and I strain to hear him for background noise. 'I'm at the Laughing Pig,' he says. 'Do you fancy joining me? Rosa and James aren't here. Apparently, they've gone to a works party.'

'I wouldn't be the best company, Mason. 'I'm not feeling one hundred percent to be honest.'

'Oh, what's up?'

'It's hard to say, I'm just a bit under the weather. I was sick yesterday morning and the same again today. It's probably just a virus.'

There is a momentary silence, then, 'Grace you're not pregnant, are you?'

Briefly I am stunned to silence. 'No,' I laugh awkwardly. 'It's not that. I can't get pregnant.'

'Right, ok, how about we meet at the pub tomorrow for lunch. That's if you feel up to it?'

'Sounds great. I doubt I'll be eating anything though.'

Chapter 43

My wits have been as taut as a noose's knot, waiting for Tenwyn's attendance. It is not until the afternoon after my argument with Matilda that he finally appears, ambling in with a smile and courteously removing his cap with a slight bow.

'Sir, my fears are allayed to see you again.' I rush to him, then counter myself. I should like to throw my arms about his neck and weep upon his shoulder, but etiquette restrains me. His demeanour appears 'ere calm, even as I apprise him of Matilda's menacing threats.

'Are you not troubled?' I ask, a little irked by his stillness. 'Do you not see that she has as good as accused you and your family of the grim charge of witchcraft?'

Tenwyn leans forward in his chair. 'I have notable standing in these parts Elizabeth. It is not possible to make sense of the customs here in Cornwall unless one is born and bred here. We are lone wolves cossetting ourselves away from the rest of the kingdom, adhering to our own traditions and folklore that have been passed down the generations with vigour and pride. Outsiders may believe our accounts of giants, mermaids and piskies are mere tales for their children, but the lore is in our blood, woven into the very psyche of our folk. We have a strong heritage, even setting down our own laws, much to the chagrin of others, and it is no great surprise that we are often regarded with suspicion.

No local magistrate would condemn me here, for there is no charge to answer.'

'Yet it would be foolish sir to misjudge Matilda's mastery. She has the cunning of the fox quite capable of outwitting any hunting party. She aims to supplant you with another physician. Trust me Tenwyn, she is a force not to be reckoned with.'

'You are most gracious in your concern my lady.' He looks at me kindly with pale blue eyes. 'In hindsight I am not surprised, since I scorned Matilda by rebuffing her advances.'

I am aghast. 'You too? It would appear that she seeks to be attended by every gentleman, even as she goes about professing adoration for her absent husband.'

'Aye, I do believe she wishes to be desired amongst all men.'

I shake my head, my mood matching the ferocity of orange flames dancing wildly in the fire. 'I am at my wits end. She has sent the chaplain to my door, threatens to advise my husband that I am bedevilled and in need of sanctity and now she has torn William from my bosom.' Unwanted angry tears fill my eyes.

Tenwyn looks at me steadily. 'I know you are aggrieved Elizabeth, yet they are both treacherous and wanton, making a good match for each other. Your eyes still deceive you, for William is not what you conceive him to be. His purpose shall always reside in his next conquest.'

'Your words do sting sir, yet I am beginning to taste the truth from them. I am aware that my urge for affection steered me onto a false path and I was a dolt for believing his troth was faithful,' I say bitterly.

I am arrested by a sudden urge to vomit, hastening to the garderobe forthwith, then retching from the pit of my stomach. Shouting out to Mary, I bid she bring herb-infused water to me, to wash before returning to William.

'Pray excuse me, I have felt quite unwell these past few days. Perhaps there is something you may do for me?' I ask him.

'I shall be pleased to examine you. Was this the first time you have vomited?'

'Nay, it first occurred yesterday upon waking.'

'And are there any other signs?'

'Just a general malaise and nausea.'

He has me lay on the bed and gently probes my stomach with his fingers. 'Is there any tenderness?'

'Yes, a little there below my navel.'

'Do you ever feel any internal movement here?'

'No, not as such, just a slight discomfort.'

Tenwyn next examines my urine, mixing it with a little wine, then he sits in his chair by the fire. He begins to toy with his beard, deep in thought, then looks up. 'Can you recount when you last had your courses?' he asks.

'Oh, I am not able to recall, though not for a number of weeks.'

He pauses for reflection, now looking a little concerned, which draws an unease to my own senses.

'May you tell me what you have found sir?'

He looks at me steadily. 'Elizabeth, I believe you may be with child.'

Chapter 44

The Laughing Duck is teaming with university students again. It always surprises me why they all come here when they have their own campus where they can get cheaper drinks. Thankfully Mason arrived early and has managed to secure us a table. He looks up from his phone and greets me warmly. 'I've ordered myself a sandwich, would you like one?'

'No thank you, I'm still feeling queasy. It's my turn to get the drinks though.' I fight my way to the bar, brushing past rude students who refuse to move, and end up feeling quite light-headed. By the time I get back to Mason, he is halfway through his sandwiches.

He looks up. 'I'm sorry if I scared you yesterday, asking if you were pregnant. It was tactless of me.'

'No worries,' I shrug. 'It sent a shiver for a moment, but I think my accident put to bed any prospects of me ever getting pregnant. We're going to try IVF when Lawrence gets back. Can you imagine him coming home and seeing me with a bump?' I laugh. 'It's not like I could pass it off as his, as he's been away too long.'

'Yes, it just sounded a bit like morning sickness the way you described it.'

'I can see that because I've only really been sick in the mornings, but that's just coincidence. I must have picked up a bug from somewhere.'

I tell him about Rosa's unwelcome visit, and like me, he thinks she has an audacity vying for both my approval and friendship for having stolen my boyfriend.

'You don't need friends like that,' says Mason. 'She always seems very friendly. I didn't realise she was like that.'

'Yes, too many people are fooled by her.'

Mason looks at his watch. 'Damn,' he says, 'sorry love, I must dash off again. I won't kiss you goodbye, in-case you give me the lurgy.' He rushes out the door shouting, 'get better soon,' behind him.

I arrive home to find the house has been tidied and am embarrassed to see Margot in the kitchen washing up last night's pans. 'Oh, hi Margot, you're back,' I say stupidly.

'Yes madam.'

'How is your mum?'

'Better than she was, thank you madam.' It's like getting blood out of a stone having a conversation with Margot, but at least I don't have to spend much time with her. I am pissed-off that she's back so soon, though I shall no longer have to concern myself with smuggling James out the house each morning.

Still feeling jaded, I decide to have a hot bath with lots of bubbles, sea salt and essential oils.

Luxuriating in the warm foam and fragrant scents, I sink deep into relaxation and the mirror appears to my inner vision like clockwork. It seems a little hazy today, taking a-while to clear. Then I see Elizabeth, who appears to be leaning over something. On closer inspection, it is a hole hewn in stone, something like an archaic toilet. I watch as she retches and vomits several times. Her maid is standing by with a basin of water, strewn with lavender heads and other herbs. The depiction is short-lived, becoming hazy, then disappearing altogether.

Chapter 45

I am tremulous tottering on my feet, my entire body jolted by the blow, sitting quickly to arrest a fall. 'Nay sir,' I say to Tenwyn. 'What you say is quite inconceivable. Edward and I have been bidding for a child for years, yet the lord has deemed me unsuited to the task. Edward 'ere chastises me of my failure.'

Tenwyn looks on me kindly. 'It is unjust for a man to charge a woman so, when the failing may lie within his own constitution. For centuries, male pride has set the blame at the door of his spouse, but oftentimes this may be found to be a cruel misjudgement.'

I rise to my feet. 'Sir, pray dwell further on your forecast, for if you are right, then I am doomed.' I watch Tenwyn tousle with his beard as he contemplates, and all of a sudden, my head starts to spin, and I become unsteady on my feet. Then all is black.

When I open my eyes, I find I am in my bed with Tenwyn watching over me. 'Where's your beard?' I ask. He looks bemused and then I see it is there as always. 'It's still here,' he says, playfully touching it with his fingers.

'Forgive me, I do believe I must be quite mad, for your face changed again, as before.' I roll my eyes while shaking my head. 'No matter, I am quite giddy. What happened, why am I abed?'

'You fainted, that is all.'

I sit up, at once recollecting what had occurred. I look to Tenwyn saying imploringly 'pray, tell me you were mistaken sir. Edward has been away for too long for a child to have been gotten by him. Oh, mother of Mary forgive me, what could this mean?' I cross myself.

Tenwyn becomes aware of my maid, quickly dismissing her, that she may not be privy to any further confidences, though I fear she may already have been availed of too much. He finds my wrap and places it gently about my shoulders. Then he leans over me uttering in a soft voice, 'I am not able to confirm it absolutely Elizabeth, but the signs are there, and you should prime yourself. We shall wait a little longer.'

I shake my head wildly. 'Nay, for my stomach shall swell and my plight shall be there for all to see!' I exclaim.

'Tenwyn rests his hand on my shoulder, 'still yourself Elizabeth,' he says.

'Nay I may not wait sir. What am I to do, there must be some potion or other that you possess?'

'Pray, do calm yourself my lady. There is a wise woman I have heard of, Agnes. She is known to assist in these affairs. I shall seek her out.'

I clutch hold of his arm roughly. 'Pray, not a word. No one must hear of this,' I whisper. I think of the maid and what she may have gleaned. She appears to be more loyal than Henriette, who I believe was paid off by Matilda, and I must lay my trust in God that I may not be betrayed again by a servant.

Chapter 46

My head is foggy from worry and a lack of sleep, and my feet are icy cold, as I drag myself out of bed. Again, I feel queasy as I make my way to the kitchen to put the kettle on. It has now been a week since the vomiting began and my condition hasn't really changed. I'm still being sick in the mornings, then picking up in the afternoons, albeit a little low on energy. Mason's comments about morning sickness have been playing on my mind and I am beginning to wonder if he may have been right. Consequently, I have been mulling it over all night, switching from the notion that I might be pregnant as ridiculous, to the raw facts of it being a symptomatic match. Either way, I need to find out sooner rather than later.

It takes me a long time to get ready and I know I am procrastinating. The next hour or so is a bit of a blur as I stumble home with a small package of destiny, purchased over the counter at the chemist.

The instructions are clear, almost too easy to be true. It's a simple case of dipping the stick in urine and if the tip reveals two blue lines after three minutes, the result is positive and only one line, negative. I make myself a cup of tea to reflect on it all first, as so much hangs on the outcome. I convince myself that the result will be negative, but a small voice in the background asks how, having yearned to be pregnant for so long, I would feel if it were positive? For I have long believed it would never be possible, that it would ever remain an unfulfilled dream. But I have no choice but to be governed by the voice of reason, that if positive, it would be the outcome of an adulteress affair and born of a man who is unworthy of being a father. And so, I would have to have an abortion. End of story.

My hands are shaking as I follow the instructions and the three minutes seem endless as I stare at the stick. I take a sharp intake of breath when two blue lines show and check the leaflet to make sure I have carried out the instructions correctly.

Grabbing my bag and keys, I drive quickly back to the chemist to purchase another kit, for I must have made a mistake, a little miffed that I have wasted my money.

'I know it says on the packet these tests are 99% accurate, but are they really?' I ask the lady behind the counter. 'Yes, they are,' she says. 'Didn't you buy one earlier?'

'Yes, but I want to make sure,' I reply. She raises her eyebrows, then smiles, saying, 'well, good luck.'

Chapter 47

I carefully climb the steep stone steps, raising my skirts to avoid tripping should I step upon them. On reaching the top, a cool rush of air brushes against my face, as I step out onto the turret. A young guard is slumped against the wall caught in a nap. My sudden appearance arrests his attention and he quickly rises to his feet. I have scant time for the castle guards, for they have a propensity to be un-clean, foul-mouthed, and ill-educated. 'Go,' I say. 'Plainly you have a hankering for sleep, be gone to repose your wearisome self.' He appears peeved that I should presume he would do my bidding. 'I am at my duty, my lady,' he retorts. It vexes me that the guards pay such little reverence to nobility, save to those who employ them.

I tut. 'It appears that you are not! I shall be answerable to your constable, that you are acting on a lady's will to breathe a little fresh air in comfort.' The guard stands firm and I find his obstinacy galling. 'Then I shall apprise him of your idleness on the watch as well as your insubordinate behaviour,' I pronounce, and he finally abdicates, scuttling off and leaving me to ponder on the declining calibre of servants these days.

I take a long deep breath, smelling salt carried on the air all the way from the sea. It is bright and sunny yet with a penetrating chill. Upon waiting for Tenwyn's return, my nerves have felt like a loom maiden's entangled threads.

The purging has tailed off a little, some days being worse than others, yet the nausea and fatigue ensues.

To take my mind from my predicament, I have become accustomed to studying the castle activities down below. Two wagons are crossing the drawbridge with their supplies, a maid is hanging laundry in the courtyard and soldiers are practising their archery skills in the castle grounds. Yet no distraction may assuage thoughts of my death knell. I pace up and down, just as I have been in my chamber all morning. 'Oh, where is Tenwyn? Is he not aware of the urgency of this matter?' I shout out.

Yet it is not until the following day that he finally comes, and I bombard him as he enters my chamber. 'Oh, where have you been Tenwyn, my wits are drawn?'

'Pray, still yourself Beth,' he says, beckoning me to be seated. 'Forgive me, for I had to seek out Agnes, then wait for her to prepare her potion. She is a gnarly woman and not one to be hastened. One of the plants is not accessible in this season, so she had to seek out another.' He appears a little rasped and I regret my harassment.

'Forgive me Tenwyn,' I say more softly, 'for I am overwrought.' Mary presents us both with a tankard of ale. She is proving to be a more faithful maid than Henriette and I am glad of her.

'Have there been any changes in your condition?' he asks.

'Nay sir, the purging is a little less now, yet the nausea persists.' Tenwyn examines my stomach again and I still feel a slight discomfort where he places his fingers.

'What think you sir?' I ask afterwards.

'My prognosis remains unchanged,' he says solemnly, and I look down at my lap forlornly.

He reaches into his bag, bringing forth a small bottle containing a thick brown-green liquid with bits in it that resemble pieces of bark. I find myself grimacing, turning my head away. 'It looks putrid,' I remark ungraciously.

'Yes, but Agnes assures me it shall do the trick. You must ingest the entire bottle at sun-up, and then the same the following day. I have four of these bottles, but Agnes claims that three should be sufficient.' The thought alone is enough to make me want to retch. 'And what should I expect?' I ask hesitantly.

'There will be pain in your stomach, and you shall bleed heavily. I fear you shall be unwell for a spell.' He looks at me soberly. 'Gird yourself Elizabeth, for this may be a perilous course. Agnes cautioned to take as few of the bottles as possible, as too much may poison you.' He appears a little uneasy as he places the bottles on the table. 'Are you quite sure you want to go through with this? Perhaps we should give it more time to see if you really are with child?'

I shake my head despondently. 'Lamentably sir, I have no cause to doubt your forecast. I have missed my courses and the twinges in my belly deems to affirm it. Though I appeal to Mother Mary to pray tell me why it may not be the long yearned-for child of my wedlock, in place of a rogue of a man who has no care? My poor judgement has led me down this unholy path and God has determined this to be my retribution.' I cross myself fearfully and Tenwyn follows suit.

Chapter 48

'Thanks for coming over. I really need someone to talk to right now.'

Masons perches himself on the arm of the sofa. 'Oh, please don't tell me James wants you back.'

'No, I haven't heard from him. I can hardly believe he was whispering sweet nothings only two weeks ago and now it's as though we never even existed.'

'I'm sorry Grace, but you'll soon see it's a blessing in disguise. So, what's up then?'

'I'm pregnant!'

'Oh shit, really?' Mason looks shocked.

'Well, I can hardly believe it myself, but two tests have given a positive result and they are reputed to be 99% accurate.'

'Look I'm not prying, but I suppose it has to be James?'

'Shit Mason, what do you think I am? I don't sleep around you know. Of course, it is his.'

He takes out his small tin of tobacco and papers and begins the laborious process of constructing a thin smoke.

'I know, I know. I'm sorry. I thought it might be your husband's, but he's obviously been away for too long. What are you going to do?'

'Well put it this way, Lawrence would probably kill me if he came home to find me carrying another man's child. And James is a good for nothing little shit, who can't even take care of himself, let alone a child.'

'So, ok, I take it you'll be having an abortion?'

I look down trying to hide the tears forming in my eyes, but I know it's impossible concealing anything from Mason. He comes to me and I surrender in his arms, unleashing stored-up vulnerability. Mason comforts me as a parent would a child, feeling safe in protective arms.

I quickly compose myself, venturing into the bathroom to wipe away the smeared mascara from my cheeks and tidy up. Then I put my coat on and join Mason on the patio. I personally have felt no compulsion to smoke lately, which I think must be a sub-conscious impulse of preservation for the baby.

'I'm sorry Grace, my mention of abortion stung, didn't it?' Mason hits the bullseye again.

'I know it must be done, but it hurts you know. Lawrence and I have wanted a baby for so long. Every time my period started, I was devastated and then it would be a long wait for the next month, to be disappointed all over again. Month after month, year after year we tried, and then as soon as I took my eye off the ball thinking it was impossible, bingo, it happened, but at the wrong damn time! It's hard to describe Mason, but when you've wanted a baby for so long and you get pregnant, a part of you really wants to hang onto it. Whenever I think about an abortion my body goes into panic. I imagine the baby saying *please don't get rid of me*. It's ridiculous, but my instinct seems to be screaming at me not to do it.'

Mason looks at me with his kind eyes. 'I understand Grace, I really do. I will support you in whatever you decide. If you want to keep it, you will either have to be straight with Lawrence, or walk away from your marriage. You also need to consider James. As the father, he does have a right to know.'

'Huh, you think so?' I can't even contemplate this at the moment, still reeling from the way he's treated me. 'If I were to have an abortion, do you think God would punish me and not give me a second chance?'

'I'm not religious, so I'm the wrong one to ask, but from my perspective I would disagree. It's more likely you would punish yourself on a sub-conscious level if you felt guilty about it.'

'Well, I have an appointment with the doctor tomorrow, so I will discuss it with her.'

'Well, let me know how it goes, ok? Are you still experiencing the sickness?'

'It's ongoing and it's horrible but I can live with it. Interestingly, I've seen Elizabeth being sick and I'm wondering if she is also pregnant, bearing in mind all the synchronicities that seem to be occurring across both timelines. Just imagine the ramifications for her if she is. I doubt abortions were easy to come by back then.'

'No, it doesn't bear thinking about.'

'She seems so alone, and I sometimes give her imaginary hugs and I know you won't believe me, but it's as if she can feel it because I catch her shuddering. And I'm sure she catches a glimpse of me sometimes. But Mason, what I don't understand is that my accident may have opened up my own psychic abilities to see her, but how is it possible the other way round, that she might be able to see me?'

'I know, it's hard to grasp, but as I see it, you are both so closely aligned in your consciousness, that it seems reasonable that you are able to influence each other. It sounds like she too is psychic, perhaps even acquiring that from you. For all we know, we may all be affected by our other selves, past and present, but are just not aware of it. Who knows?'

'Yes, I keep forgetting that we are the same soul having experiences in different bodies.' I smile at him, rise from my chair, and open my arms out wide. 'Elizabeth has the doctor and I have you. Thank you, Mason,' I say embracing him fondly.

Chapter 49

I awaken before my maid, a little ahead of sun-up, with a woolly head and ice-cold feet. I quietly get out of bed and make my way to the table bearing my needlework basket, wherein Agnes's potion lies, hidden beneath a cloth. Taking hold of the bottle, I am all of a sudden overcome with nausea and hasten to the garderobe, arriving just in time to vomit. I hear a gasp from Mary and, before I know it, she is there standing behind me with the basin of herb water and a cloth. When I think the purging has ceased, my stomach brings forth more. The bile makes me cough and I stagger past Mary to the chair and sit catching my breath. Mary hands me the wet cloth, a concerned look on her face. 'Shall I summon the physician my lady?' she asks.

'No, I am fine now,' I say composing myself. I think of the bottle of potion still sitting on the shelf. It shall have to wait now until the morrow.

Later that morning I am gladdened by a visitation from my priest from Suffolk, Father John. 'I am so pleased to see you Father,' I say, crossing myself. He is quite unlike Father Arthur in both appearance and temperament, young and lean, with the inclination to smile on occasion. He is far too comely for a man of the cloth.

'And you, Elizabeth, forgive me that it took so long, but I have had important business to attend to at the Priory of Saints.'

'Tell me, is the ague still raging?'

'It has taken its toll I'm afraid, especially in the villages, the poor being amongst the worst affected. It is beginning to phase out, though there is talk now of the plague advancing itself from Europe to the south coast, causing frenzy and mayhem. I understand that many of the nobility are already planning their retreats to the north.'

'Ah, such sorrow,' I muse. 'It would seem my fate is sealed, that I shall reside in this monstrous place for an eternity.'

Father John shakes his head. 'Do not forsake your blessings Elizabeth, for the good lord has smiled upon you, being free from peril, sheltered within the comfort of these walls.'

Fittingly admonished, I select my words with caution. 'You are right Father of course and I am ever grateful to my husband's brother for his hospitality, I assure you. Yet it is so difficult here away from my own kith and kin with no household to run, with few friends to call my own. The Cornish you know have curious superstitions, which is quite disconcerting. I am quick to temper; a fact you are wise to I believe?' Father John smiles in acknowledgment. 'Well, many arrows have been hurled at me here and ludicrous presumptions have reached the door of the castle chaplain, that I am a frenzied woman with demons hiding beneath my robes. Father Arthur seeks to dispatch me to the priory for sanctity.'

Father John listens intently. 'On whose authority?'

'He has the backing of Lady Matilda and seeks to appeal to Edward since I have set my own refusal.'

'And how do you think your husband shall respond?'

'As you know Father, sentiment amongst us is lacking, and I trust that he would put Father Arthur's word above my own. Indeed, he would be glad to extricate me from his life, that he may seek another to beget him an heir, where I have failed.'

'I understand your precarious position, Elizabeth.' There is warmth in his words, and I watch as he interlocks his fingers, deep in thought. 'Yet I am ill-placed to countermand the chaplain here, so do not know how best I may serve you.'

I stop myself from nervously toying with my wedding band. 'It troubles me that I have not partaken in the confession for a-while, as I may not count on the confidence. All I ask is that you permit me to confess to you, being a man whom I may trust.'

'Well, we would need to gain permission from Father Arthur first.'

'In this he would decline and seek to punish me further.'

Father John sighs. 'Very well, I shall aim to arrange it at the church in town on the morrow.'

I bow my head in supplication. 'Thank you, Father. Please pray for me and my sins.' He reaches into his bag for his tools and I rise to my feet to receive his blessing.

When he leaves, I sigh with relief that I may at last absolve myself, collapsing on my bed verily fatigued of my burdens.

Chapter 50

This morning I prayed for the first time in years. I believe in God but not from a Christianity viewpoint. When I had my near-death experience, I was not met by angels, though I experienced a blissful feeling, impossible to put into words. I dutifully attended church with my grandparents, who were devout Catholics, up until the age of fourteen, when I opted out. I found it sombre and boring, failing to understand the necessity of praying with others in a designated building, when you can do it in the privacy of your own home. I am quite sure that I am not the only one to seek spiritual solace in times of trouble and it may seem selfish, but the God I believe in is all-wise, forgiving and understanding of our weaknesses.

Lawrence's calls continue to be discouraging as he off-loads his aches and pains, stresses, and irritations. Faced with my own current predicament, I am already too stressed to take on anymore and have come to dread the sound of my mobile. I can often tell when he has been drinking, not because he slurs his words, as he never does, but by the level of his aggression. Sometimes he rings several times a day, checking up on me, wanting to know what I am doing; on and on. Increasingly I am ignoring his calls, like this morning when he woke me at 6.00am. Right now, I have more important things on my mind than my drunken neurotic husband.

Dr Hendrick welcomes me into her office without looking up from her computer. Then she swivels around to me with a well-polished professional smile, asking how she may help. She listens patiently and affirms the accuracy of over-the-counter pregnancy tests, explaining that the sample I have brought in will be sent to the laboratory for absolute confirmation. We discuss period dates and my sickness, and after a little maths, she comes up with an estimated figure of ten weeks. My mind becomes fuzzy with the dawning realization that I am actually pregnant, that up until this moment, with two confirmed tests, morning sickness and a swelling belly, I have yet been in denial of. Dr Hendrick's confirmation has taken it all to a whole new level. I hesitate when she asks of my intentions. 'I don't want to keep it,' I say under my breath, carefully dodging the word abortion.

I am sure she will have picked up on the fact that it is a choice I alone have decided on, yet she doesn't probe me on this. Despite Mason's advice, I have no intention of telling James. I shall get this thing over and done with as quickly and quietly as possible, learn from my mistakes and move on. Then when Lawrence returns, we may try again. Evidently there is nothing physically wrong with either of us conception-wise, so perhaps we have just been too tightly wrapped.

'I always advocate taking a little time to consider making the final decision before taking irreversible steps, as occasionally things aren't as straight-forward as we would like them to be,' says Dr Hendrick, with her well-polished smile.

'Such as what?' I ask.

'Every situation is different. In some cases, there are pressures from partners or family members. Sometimes there is a change of heart and some women are fearful or find the idea of a termination an emotional experience. It always pays to keep an open mind and to be aware that there are other options worth considering, like adoption.'

'Will it affect my chances of becoming pregnant again?'

'Providing the termination is straight-forward, no. Most women who've had a termination, whether medical or surgical, go on to have healthy babies when they are ready, without any difficulties.'

I do not hear all that she is saying, for my mind is conflicted. A sense of wonder and excitement keeps re-surfacing, to quickly be pushed back down again. Even though I may never again have this opportunity, it is wrong in every sense. It is the result of a loveless adulteress relationship, and holds the destiny card to cease my marriage, setting me on an unknown path. It is imperative that the deed be done quickly before I begin to feel it growing in my belly.

Carefully concealing my true feelings with an appearance of composure, I thank Dr Hendrick, leaving the room calmly, but inwardly a small voice is screaming.

Chapter 51

As I walk from the gloom of the church into bright winter sunshine, I feel a heavy burden has been relieved from my slight shoulders. I have confessed my sins and prayed for grace and forgiveness. God spoke to me in my contemplative moments bowed at the altar, instructing me to be more diligent in my spiritual practice; to daily attend chapel, study my bible and recite the litanies. I am shameful that I have neglected these duties and vow to become a more devout servant.

My conscience is clear, and I have God on my side, but there is still the matter of somehow ridding myself of this burden within my belly, the physical manifestation of my sin and guilt, sent by the good lord not as a gift from heaven, but as punishment for my ills.

I abstained from taking the potion this morning since Tenwyn warned it would make me ill, which would prevent me from attending church with Father John for this vital confession. Again, I vomited upon rising and Mary dutifully brought me the basin. I have informed her that I have gotten a sickness, though I suspect she is by now apprised of the truth.

Father John made his departure straight back to the priory in Suffolk, bearing the heavy coined purse I gave him. Nothing goes unnoticed here, and I wonder if we were observed riding into town together. No doubt a story shall have been concocted, a diversion to lighten an afternoon's humdrum for the needlework circle. Approaching the drawbridge as I return, proud upon my fine man of a horse, I sense hostile eyes looking down from the high windows of this frosty castle, for it is from there those spies make gossip and mischief.

As soon as I return to my chamber, I open the big chest containing my gowns and dig to the bottom, seeking out my bible and little book of litanies and set myself down before the fire.

As I begin to read, I feel a sudden coldness about me, even though the fire is raging, and it seems as though there is a presence, yet the chamber is empty. I look all about nervously, then feeling something upon my shoulder, I leap from my chair crying out, and Mary comes running to my side.

Chapter 52

My day dream is interrupted by Margot, creeping in in her house pumps with polish and duster at hand. 'Please don't bother doing the living room today,' I say, and without a word she turns and leaves. With great reluctancy I pick up the leaflet from the coffee table that Dr Hendrick gave me and begin to read. It would seem there are two forms of termination, the first being a pill that induces a miscarriage, which is best carried out before ten weeks. The other option, which would no doubt apply to me, is a minor surgical procedure. It all sounds so simple on paper, yet just by reading about it, I am overcome with sadness. The dream I have longed for has manifested, residing comfortably here within my belly, and yet I am considering its destruction. I rest my hands protectively on my stomach. People have abortions every day of the week, all over the world. I must toughen-up, be more pragmatic and get on with it.

As if he picked up on my sadness over the airways, Mason calls me. His tender voice has a calming effect and he promises to call on me after work. I sink back into the sofa, drawing the blanket over my head, exhausted from a lack of sleep. I wonder about Elizabeth. If my suspicions are right, that she too is pregnant, it will be far worse for her if it is out of wedlock, as I imagine it would be. For one thing it's unlikely she shall have the support of her peers, and I wonder if abortions were even possible in those days; if so, were they safe? The sobering thought gives me the perspective I need to stop from feeling sorry for myself. I am blessed to have the backing of my GP, confident that it will be conducted in a safe environment and will all be behind me in just a few weeks' time.

I wonder if the mirror will offer any insights today? It takes me longer than usual to gain any clarity, most likely due to the state of my mind. But I persevere, concentrating on the relaxation exercises and when the mirror eventually manifests, I am instantly drawn in to an image of Elizabeth kneeling at the altar in church. Her head is bowed, and she appears very pious. The church looks different to the one she normally attends, a lot bigger.

I start to the sound of my mobile, rousing me harshly back to the room. It stops as soon as I pick it up and I see the caller was James. I am about to return the call when he rings again, and I wait for him to open up the conversation.

'Grace?'

'Yes?'

'Are you ok?

'What do you care?' I retort bitterly.

'It's just I've heard something.'

'What?'

'You're not pregnant, are you?'

Chapter 53

I have endured another troublesome night, my mind tormented by fear, strange visions, and imaginings. Mary is at my bedside. 'I do not wish to waken you my lady, but the bells shall soon be chiming for prime.' I groan aloud, already feeling nauseous, tempted to abstain from chapel this morning, yet I have vowed to God to be a more devout servant.

As I dress, I am anguished to find my bodice too snug, even now in need of adjustment. Yet another opportunity of drinking that dreadful potion has been missed and time is pressing. If only I were permitted to take it later in the day when I feel less nausea, but Tenwyn was emphatic in his directive that it must be consumed at sun-up.

As ever, the little chapel is over-peopled. Candles in abundance throw dancing shadows against the walls and the strong aroma of incense arouses my nausea 'ere more. We take our places, the family being last, then Father Arthur leads the choristers up the aisle, chanting their doleful anthem. Once seated, there is a lengthy silence before Father Arthur launches into a recital from his great bible.

I fidget in discomfort of an over-tight bodice and nausea exacerbated by the pungent incense aroma. If only I had stayed abed as my fatigued body had advised. I listen not to the dreary monologue, for Father Arthur has ardour neither in heart nor voice. William is at the end of the pew in front of me, upstanding in his black velvet doublet and cap, his wavy hair draping down the back of his neck. He must have felt my scowl levelled at his back, for he turns his head glancing at me over his shoulder. I shudder, musing at his prowess in his terse switching from amorous lover to aloof detachment. Just as Tenwyn had foreseen, I have been merely a target in his game of archery. Whereas I have to bear my guilt and sin within my very body, William has no effect or recompense and is free to proceed with his dalliances. Why does God punish women more than men? Why should they bear all the burdens, whilst the men are granted to walk the other way?

I wonder if I should inform William that I bear his child? In truth I desire never to speak to him again, for the dolt that I have become because of his making. It is seeming that he would laugh, since it is his way to assume a jest in all things. Assuredly he would show no grace, likely refuting it was of his own making. More disastrously, he would apprise Matilda, who may bid Edward. No, it would be a foolish deed, an aim for another arrow to my eye.

I solemnly take my place kneeling before the altar awaiting the Eucharist. I am uncomfortable and longing to return to my chamber, though Father Arthur adopts no haste.

My stomach feels unsettled and I become aware of bile quickly arising, evoking an urgent desire to vomit. I cover my face with one hand, the other upon my stomach and rise quickly to my feet, gather my skirts and run forthwith from the chapel to the nearest garderobe, leaving behind echoing gasps from the faithful flock.

Chapter 54

There is a stunned silence as I digest James's question. How could he possibly know that I am pregnant? I have told no one except Mason.

'James, I haven't heard from you for three weeks. You dropped me like a hot brick and now you ring out of the blue like this. What are you on about?' I bluff.

'That's typical of you Grace, coming across as Little Miss Innocent. If you're pregnant, I want to know if it's his or mine?'

I pause, trying to keep myself calm. 'James, I don't know what you're talking about.'

'That bloke you're with.'

I laugh, 'excuse me?'

'Mason.'

'Actually James, I am not *with* Mason. He is just a friend.'

'Whatever. Well Eva overheard him on the phone the other night asking you if you were pregnant. Everyone's talking about it.'

At first, I am taken aback, and then I recall my conversation with Mason when I told him about my sickness, and he asked me if I was pregnant. He said he was in the pub at the time, so it's quite likely he was overheard.

'Oh, they are, are they? Well, you can tell them all from me that I am *not*. I'm sure they will all be disappointed at the news. Whilst you're about it, you can tell that girlfriend of yours she is welcome to you!' With that, I hang up before he is able to reply.

Mason is devastated to think that he is responsible for setting off the rumour, but I reassure him that I understand it was a genuine mistake.

'I'm coming with you,' he says drawing on his cigarette. He notices my non-plus expression and continues. 'I want to come with you when you have the abortion.'

'Ah thanks, you have no idea how much that means to me,' I say, relieved not to have to endure it all alone.

He looks at me quizzically. 'Are you definitely going to go through with it?'

'Of course. I have to.'

'And you're not going to tell James?'

'No, I want to do this without him. Telling him would be like reporting to the whole community. No one can know about any of this.' I look at him affirming the importance of his confidentiality.

'It's okay, your secret's safe with me,' he says, and I believe him.

'So, what's the next step?'

'I have to go for a consultation at the clinic and then I'm hoping to get a date.'

'How have your visions been going?'

'Well, it appears that Elizabeth is going through a similar experience, but it must be so much more difficult for her. You were saying recently that everything happens for a reason and I've been trying to work out what this is all about? Do you think I am supposed to be doing something, like helping her in some way?'

'Who knows Grace? I wish I had the answers. All I would say is that right now your main responsibility is to yourself. Perhaps you should have a rest from all that for a-while, because it's important that you are rooted in the present at the moment.'

I understand his rationale, but do not think that I am capable of letting it go, not now. I feel I have a duty to Elizabeth. Disconnecting from her would feel like a betrayal. What's more it would seem as if I were losing a part of myself. On some level I need her, and I feel she needs me.

She is in church again, kneeling just as before, waiting for the Eucharist. At first I think I am viewing the same scene as yesterday, but I notice it's her regular chapel this time, much smaller and over-crowded. She looks serene with her head inclined patiently waiting for the priest. But she rises all of a sudden, holding fast her stomach and runs, as the rest of the congregation stare after her in disbelief. I set the intention to stay with her and then see her leaning over a stone toilet, clutching her stomach, and vomiting. She pushes back her long braid behind her and retches again. Poor Elizabeth, how humiliating it must have been running from church like that.

When the vomiting has ceased, she stands back upright and I imagine giving her a bear hug. It grieves me to witness what she is going through and being powerless to help her. This is all I can do, yet on some level, I sense she knows she is not alone, and I too seek comfort in that knowledge.

Chapter 55

I am mortified to have caused such a charade in church, of all the places. Had I purged myself there before his faithful flock, it would have affirmed Father Arthur's conviction that I am entranced by demons. Now charged to make a play of it, I get myself abed post-haste. Shortly after, Matilda arrives with her physician in tow. She feigns concern for me, rushing to my bedside. 'You gave us such a scare Elizabeth,' she says, 'what came over you?'

'I felt the need to purge,' I reply sombrely. 'Forgive me for obstructing the sermon, but I was quite incapable of fending it off.'

'This is Richard, our new physician. He is from London, more accomplished than the local physicians, who depend on age-old concoctions cobbled together by their ancestors.'

'Pray do not find me ungracious Matilda, yet I hold countless esteem for Master Tenwyn, for he has always tended me well.' *Matilda is unequivocally vexed, her mask beginning to falter. She glances at Richard, who grimaces slightly.*

'He is amiable, yet such an attribute is no qualification for competence. Richard is a man of sound stature and he shall investigate you thoroughly.' *With that she is gone, and I look anxiously at Master Richard, a tall man with dark hair and grey beard.*

'My lady, I shall proceed by testing your waters,' *he says searching his bag for a piss pot. I recoil in horror as he also* brings forth a pot of leeches. 'Nay sir pray do not bleed me,' I say demurely.

Master Richard smiles, yet his eyes reveal nought but coldness. 'My lady, the leeching is necessary to stabilise your humours.'

I shuffle uncomfortably. 'Master Tenwyn, my own physician, counters it is not a mandatory practice,' I say indignantly.

'Well, I should inquire as to his efficacy, for bleeding is esteemed amongst all eminent physicians, whereas superstition and folklore I fear are not.' His disposition is most irksome, having neither courtesy nor warmth amongst his tools, as does Tenwyn. He sets about examining my urine; the colour, smell, and taste, concluding from it that I am to drink more ale. Then he bleeds me with his terrifying leeches, writhing over my body, biting with their tiny sharp teeth, until my blood has filled enough of Master Richard's cups for his satisfaction.

By the time he has left, I am light-headed and fatigued, glad to be left to repose. Yet as soon as I close my eyes, I am faced with a strange seeing. I observe the lady in odd attire that I have seen before. She appears to be leaning over something and I watch as she gags and purges into a large vessel. I ponder that the poor lady's plight is akin to my own, then find myself drifting fast into a deep comforting abyss.

I am awakened by the sound of bells, which must mean it is dinner time. I beckon Mary to bring me bread and ale, for my appetite is yet poor, also instructing her to summon Tenwyn. I must presume that he has been expelled from his chambers and returned to his family's lodgings in town since he has been usurped by Master Richard. I wonder how he shall fare, now that his employ has been drawn from him. I cannot help *but wonder if it is Matilda's antipathy towards me that has been the cause of this ill-fate.*

Chapter 56

'It's done and now there's no going back.' I say to Mason on the phone.
'Oh?'
'I've had my appointment about the termination, as they call it. They don't like the word *abortion* apparently. To me, both are equal, but there you go. So, I have a date for two weeks' time, Thursday, 25th, at 11.30.'
'Ok, I'll see what I can do.'
'First though, they want to do an ultrasound to confirm the dates and check the position of the foetus.'
'Oh, how do you feel about that?'
'Apprehensive if I'm honest. The nurse told me the staff would be discreet and it's my choice whether or not to view, but it would all just add to the torture. They will be taking a good look at the child I am going to murder,' I blurt out unwittingly.
I hear Mason sigh. 'I know it's hard Grace, but remember at this stage it's not fully formed, it's just a load of cells.'
'Actually, it'll be fourteen weeks by the time of the termination, the size of a lemon and beginning to look like a tiny human being.' I don't tell him how awful it was listening to all the spiel about the termination, however kind Trudy the nurse was, adeptly trying to wrap it all up into a cosy little package to make me feel at ease.

'Oh, look I'm sorry,' Mason says, 'this is all new territory to me.'

'No it's me who should be apologizing Mason, my emotions are getting the better of me. I just want the whole thing over and done with. There's no respite at the moment with raging hormones and an ever-swelling belly.'

'I get it Grace. Have you been sleeping any better?'

'Some nights yes, when I'm not having nightmares about leeches writhing all over my body, like I did last night.'

'Yeuch! Look Grace, I'm afraid I've got to get back to work. I'll pop by later if you like?'

As I hang up, I hear a clang from the kitchen. I didn't know Margot was there, believing she was upstairs. I do hope she didn't overhear our conversation.

My mobile rings. It's Lawrence.

'I've got good news Grace. I might be coming home in a couple of weeks!'

Chapter 57

'Oh Tenwyn, what a joy it is see you,' I say rushing to his side. 'It has taken but two days for my servant to seek you out.'

Tenwyn smiles warmly. 'Aye and I may be no longer welcome within these walls, but I hold allegiance to you, and if that means a small bribe at the gate, so be it.'

'I know not what I would do without you sir. That dreadful man Richard set his slimy creatures upon my body even without my consent. It was a frightful ordeal, endured in the wake of a public humiliation, when I was unwittingly pressed to leave the course of mass, since my body was roused to purge.'

Tenwyn's face breaks into a smile, then he erupts into peals of laughter. I stare at him. 'It may sound to you like a parody, yet assuredly it was no jest,' I retort.

'No, pray forgive me, yet you painted such a merry picture and it is prudent to laugh in the face of adversity at times.' I yield to a smile. 'Tenwyn, I so admire your skill of turning life's strife's into trifles.'

'What now of the other matter?' he asks more soberly.

I pause for reflection. 'I have sought to take the potion at sun-up, but it is the time when my body is disposed to the purging, and I fear I may not hold it down. Can you not petition your wise woman for another method?'

Tenwyn looks down at his hands. 'Nay my lady, you would not wish to contemplate the other way. You must proceed with that that she has proffered and wait patiently for an exacting time.'

'Yet, must I keep it down?'

'Indeed, for it shall have no efficacy if you do not.'

'Very well, I shall do as you say. I really must rid myself of this accursed thing. I have had to adjust my bodices already,' I say pointing to my stomach.

'And what of Sir William?'

'Huh, the troubadour who has journeyed to his next location! Nay sir, I have heard not a thing from him for he seeks to evade me at all costs.'

Tenwyn quietly observes the flames in the fire. 'And what shall become of you?' I ask of him.

He shrugs his shoulders. 'Mayhap I too should become a troubadour, seeking a new position.'

'Tell me of your family.'

'My mother is alone as my father and brother are away fighting. She is in poor health and I am doing my best to support her. Then I have two sisters, aged eight and five, and of course my good lady wife.'

'And so they are all reliant on you?'

'Yes.' his eyes are downcast.

'Tenwyn, when I am able to return to my home, I shall appeal to my husband to take you on.'

He looks up, 'thank you', he says softly. I go to my robe chest and search to the bottom for my purse of coins, giving him a handful. He thanks me graciously and places them in his pocket. Just then there is a loud knock and Mary appears from nowhere, pacing to the door.

I start at the sight of the person whom I least desire to see in the world; Father Arthur.

Chapter 58

My heart has been pounding ever since Lawrence told me he may be coming home sooner than expected, possibly as early as two weeks' time, around the time of the termination. I continue with my meditation each day to help calm my nerves and, despite Mason's advice, I still use the mirror to connect with Elizabeth.

Yesterday, my suspicions of her being pregnant were confirmed, as I saw her adjusting her garments. Today, her doctor friend has come to visit, and I watch as she gives him some money. There seems to be a sadness between them, as though they won't be seeing each other again. I find I am picking up more and more on Elizabeth's emotions, at times finding it hard to deal with because she seems to be in a very dark place. Damn! I am rudely awakened by the sound of the doorbell. Looking up at the clock, it would appear that Mason has arrived early.

I always feel a sense of reassurance being in the company of Mason. He is a port in a storm, having a calmness about him that seems to instil peace of mind. Today, though, after the usual pleasantries, he is on a mission to knock some sense into me.

'What you have to ask yourself is if you still love Lawrence,' he says getting straight to the crux of the matter.

'Of course; we're married. It's just that I don't like him very much at the moment.'

'Sorry Grace, that doesn't cut it. Why did you have an affair if you love him? You said yourself that you dread him coming home. Call me old fashioned, but isn't love about wanting to be with someone and missing them when you're apart?'

I hesitate, resonating with everything that he's said, but resisting nonetheless. 'Yes, but nothing's ever black and white, is it?'

'I know it's hard and you are probably nervous about losing everything, but sometimes you have to follow your nose. If things don't feel right, it's because they aren't.'

I smile. 'You are so pragmatic Mason, but it's not as simple as that. I have nowhere to go.'

'Oh, come on, it's hardly the Middle Ages,' he laughs at his Freudian slip.

'I'm sure things would be better if he would cut back on the alcohol.'

'Who are you trying to convince, me or you?' Mason asks. 'Have you ever approached him about it?'

'Yes, but he never listens. He doesn't acknowledge that he has a problem.'

'So, what will you do if he comes home before you've had the termination?'

'I doubt it'll be that quick, and anyway he will let me know when he's coming. I'll just have to keep my fingers crossed. It certainly would be awkward because the pregnancy's beginning to show now. My jeans don't fit me anymore.' I stand up and hold my stomach out to show Mason and I can tell by his face that he feels uncomfortable.

I have always been known for my obstinate staying-power, a trait I have traditionally been proud of, and yet I recognise that it can just as much be a hindrance. I take onboard all that Mason says, but don't feel ready to give up on Lawrence just yet, though we certainly have some changes to make to get back on track. When he next rings I say to him. 'When you get home, I want us to get back to where we used to be.'

'What's that supposed to mean?'

'Well, we both know we've had some rough times and we need to talk things through, but I think you should consider cutting back on your drinking.'

'Grace, you don't get it do you? I drink because you drive me to it!'

Checkmate to Lawrence ... again.

Chapter 59

Father Arthur enters rudely without invitation, regarding us both curiously. Tenwyn starts to rise from his chair, but I halt him. 'Pray sir, you may stay. Mary, fetch a chair for Father Arthur.' *She does so, yet he remains standing with his back to the fire.*

I sense he is disapproving of Tenwyn remaining with us. Receiving a tankard of ale from Mary, he examines me as though I am a thing to be had from Cheapside market. 'Elizabeth, we are most concerned for you,' *he says.* 'The affair in church was unfortunate. Are you unwell?'

Before I may respond, Tenwyn comes to my guard. 'I have examined the lady Elizabeth finding nothing serious, perchance she ingested a bad ale or stale bread. I have bidden her to rest these coming days.'

Father Arthur appears unconvinced. 'Master Tenwyn, I am bewildered to see you here. Have I been ill-advised that another has taken up your abode here?'

'That is so Father, and verily a great error of judgment set upon a man so accomplished,' *I interject.* 'Yet he is here at my behest as a good companion.'

'My lady, some may deem that professional competence may become compromised when merged with affable companionship.'

I am outraged. 'Father Arthur, I hold all due reverence for you and the church, but you have no right to judge whom I may favour as my friends.' I look at Tenwyn, who appears vexed, though prudently choosing to withhold his speech.

Father Arthur turns towards the fire rubbing his hands together, before turning back to face us. 'As God's devout servant I am charged to oversee the sanctity of the souls who dwell here and to cast out the unholy. Elizabeth, you have demonstrated much to bring grave concern to my door, that in plain sight your soul is at the mercy of bedevilment.'

Tenwyn rushes to my defence. 'Pray Father, what attestations do you hold?' he asks angrily.

'The lady has delivered many signs known to a man of the cloth. There have been countless testimonials to a display of both delirium and hallucination. Furthermore, it is known that the dark forces find God's house abhorrent and not only has Elizabeth refrained from regular attendance of chapel, but she has shied away from the sacrament of penance. The aversion was made ever clearer by her recent display of sickness during the eucharist. I fear the signs are plain for all to see.' He looks at me suspiciously. 'Possession is a pestilence to be cast out before it may infect others.'

Tenwyn stands abruptly. 'Nay sir, I have known the lady Elizabeth for some months, both as physician and companion, and avow she is none of these things. She has been but prey to menacing whispers from those who would see her fall. To my knowledge, all has been spruced up or constructed.' Never have I heard Tenwyn speak with such vigour and I am heartened by his allegiance.

Father Arthur begins to make his way to the door. 'We shall see, we shall see,' he says seemingly speaking to himself aloud. Then he turns sharply, pointing a finger at

Tenwyn. 'You should contemplate on your rank and duty sir, that is to serve your assignments with the conduct of a professional. I bid you farewell for I doubt that we shall see you within these walls again.'

Chapter 60

Wandering through the forest glade at a slow trot, Caesar and I are as one, enjoying the peace and tranquillity away from life's tribulations, noise, traffic, and people. The only sounds I can hear are organic, birds tweeting and Caesar's hooves rhythmically rustling leaves underfoot.

As we leave the forest behind us, the landscape opens up to green fields and from here on a clear day it is possible to spot the sea on the distant horizon. This is a journey that belongs to Caesar and me, one that we make every day that we are able to. The only people we usually encounter are dog walkers or runners.

As if Caesar is aroused from a trance, his ears prick suddenly at a sound and I notice a rider in the distance coming towards us. He is quite a way off, yet there is something familiar about him. As he draws closer, I realise to my surprise that it is Lawrence. I wonder what he could be doing out here, when he should be at work? I smile at him as he comes towards me, but he looks angry. I am completely at odds as to what I have done to ignite his anger.

As he draws closer, I try to lighten his mood, with a bright smile, saying 'hi, what are you doing here?' But he charges towards me, and with no forewarning, pushes me with full force, sending me flying to the ground.

I wake up in a sweat, relieved that it was all just a dream.

Chapter 61

It's been another restless night with phantoms tormenting my dreams. Mayhap Father Arthur has been right all along, that I am possessed by demons. I had a night terror that Edward returned unexpectedly, entering my chamber to find me squatting, the baby's head out midway between my legs. I awoke from the dream with a start and have since been quietly reciting the litanies I am able to recollect, whilst waiting for the first glimmer of light to peer through the small window, that I may avail myself of Agnes' dreadful potion, for I must cast this burden from my belly and soul posthaste.

It is time, so I tiptoe to my robe chest, reaching to the bottom for one of the bottles and shudder at its slimy contents. Tenwyn's instructions were to consume it all, keep it within my belly and then endure pain and ill health. It is no merry prospect, yet an imperative one. Since it is common knowledge that I am already ailing, I shall not be missed in church.

I must not dally, so I remove the stopper quickly, to be besieged by a most odious smell, causing me to retch. I hear movement, most likely Mary, and curse quietly as I had ordained to do this whilst she still slept. Without delay, I bring the bottle to my lips and swallow a mouthful. It is even more putrid than I may ever have imagined, and I feel my body repel it with a ferocity. Dropping the bottle and grasping hold of my belly, I hasten to the garderobe, arriving just in time to purge violently into the deep dark hole. And it persists on and on, the retching and purging, even when there is nought but bile to withdraw. Mary stands behind me trying to console, yet it seems there is no end to it. Finally, my body may endure no more as I feel myself sink down, collapsing in a heap upon the floor.

I awaken to the sound of voices and upon opening my eyes, I become aware of being abed, noticing Matilda and Master Richard in conference by the window. Matilda perceives I am awake and they both come over to the bed.

'So, Elizabeth, you have returned to us,' she says with a feigned smile. She is holding the remains of the empty bottle I dropped, looking at it curiously. 'Tell me, what was this potion proffered by Master Tenwyn?'

'It was a potion for my sickness,' I say quietly.

'I have told you before my dear, Master Tenwyn is an impostor and we should never have commissioned him. These local folks live still in the dark ages. Fear not, for you shall have no dealings with him again. You are now under the good care of Master Richard.'

Richard leans over me aloofly. 'My lady, pray tell me how long you have had this sickness?'

'Just a few days,' I reply.

'And is it just the mornings when you have the tendency to purge?'

'I may not be sure sir,' I say hesitantly.

'Your maid has said so,' says Matilda sardonically, throwing a look at Richard.

'Do you have tenderness within your belly?' Richard pursues.

I sit upright in bed, alerting my senses. 'Only a little. I do believe sir your prognosis was correct, that the ale was perhaps off. I am quite sure you have more important tasks to attend to. Forgive me, but all I need is time to recoup.'

'Um, perhaps several months,' muses Matilda, her eyes the colour of coal glaring at me. 'You really have no discretion Elizabeth, do you?'

'I have no idea what you are talking about.'

The castle bells begin their chiming, yet I am able to hear Matilda's words above them.

Her face is etched with malice as she says, 'your maid was privy to overhearing your parley with the imposter, Tenwyn. Elizabeth, your secret is out, you are with child!' As she marches to the door, she looks back over her shoulder insidiously. 'Expect no backing from Sir William, for he shall soon be preparing for his departure to undertake pressing duties back at his estate. Fear not, for his name shall not be disclosed.'

Chapter 62

Elizabeth vomits severely after swallowing the contents of a small bottle. Poor lady, whatever she consumed, her body doesn't like it, as the vomiting seems to go on and on until eventually, she collapses in a heap on the floor. I imagine crouching down and stroking her head as she lays there seemingly unconscious. Her maid looks to be in a panic, crying out and running off, hopefully seeking assistance. I pledge a determination to wait with her until the maid returns, which she does with the castle mistress and a man in tow. Together they lift Elizabeth, carrying her to bed, then the maid takes over, arranging the bed covers and cleaning her hands and face.

Next, the castle mistress appears to interrogate the poor maid, making her cry, then moves over to the window to consult with the man. I stay by Elizabeth's side, imagining stroking her head and see her eventually open her eyes. I pick up on her nervousness, mentally placing my hand on her shoulder for reassurance, as the woman and man approach the bed. The castle mistress is holding up the remains of the bottle that Elizabeth dropped earlier and appears to be probing her. They both look intimidating as they stand there asking Elizabeth questions and she appears to be very uncomfortable.

When they eventually leave, she holds her face in her hands in despair, and I seek to comfort her again, mentally wrapping my arms about her narrow shoulders, but today she seems oblivious to my touch. Finally, she moves her hands away from her face, clenches her fists and appears to let out a scream.

The waiting room is replete, but I manage to find a seat. My stomach feels bloated, having been instructed to drink four glasses of water, which I am required to hold onto without visiting the bathroom, until the end of the scan. I find it depressing being here amongst happy mums to be, some with their husbands in tow, excited to get a glimpse of their baby. I can't help but feel guilty being here at the other end of the spectrum and wonder if any of the other women are here with the same intentions, of ridding themselves of new life within their bellies. I realise I am sub-consciously holding my abdomen protectively and sigh deeply, determined to stick by my resolution of not sinking into the doldrums.

My name is called, and I feel sudden nausea. I follow the nurse into a room containing a lot of equipment and a bed. Another nurse introduces herself, but in my dazed state I don't register her name. My hands begin to shake as I undress and lie down on the bed. I mechanically answer the questions put to me, as a cold gel is placed on my stomach and the nurse proceeds to glide a probe around my abdomen. There is a screen facing me and images start to appear on it. The nurse says kindly that I don't have to watch, and my intention was not to, but I find myself transfixed, completely unable to avert my gaze. Most of the imagery is obscure and the nurse is diplomatic by saying very little, but I get quick glimpses of what may be a head here or a leg there. The nurse asks me something, but my mind has gone numb. She repeats the question and I quickly reclaim my senses, answering as though all is well, when in reality I am bleeding inside.

'Well, all is in order,' she says, 'nothing to worry about.' As I dismount the bed and walk from the room, I have the brief impression of wearing a long gown. For a few fleeting seconds, I am Elizabeth.

Chapter 63

Mary is quaking with fear as she stands before me and yet I am so forlorn that I have not the resolve to be overly vexed with her. 'You betrayed me. Why did you profess my confidences to Lady Matilda?' I ask her sternly.

'Forgive me my lady, I was quite unable to assist you when you fell, so I sought out Mistress Matilda. She questioned me of your condition and your audiences with Master Tenwyn. I was scared my lady, that if I did not tell her the truth, I should lose my position here.' Mary has the look of a frightened rabbit, trembling and close to tears.

'I have come to know there is not one person I may trust here in this dreadful place,' I lament, dismissing her with a wave of my hand. I draw back the bed cover and fetch my cloak and shoes, then slowly make my way up the winding stone steps to the turret for some air. I am breathless by the time I reach the top, for my body is weak and stomach tender. I failed to hold down the potion and have lost no blood, so all was in vain and seemingly I am yet with-child.

Rain courses down and howling winds cruelly lash at my face replicating God's wrath, for I have been a cause of my own demise and shall be called upon to pay the price. I see there is no escape route from this maelstrom. I stand here at the mercy of the elements, allowing the wind to toss me about and the rain to saturate, for I am quite beyond care.

When I return to my chamber I am soaked through and shivering. Mary springs into action, assisting me out of my clothes and bringing forth fresh ones. Then she sets me in front of the fire with a cup of mead. Staring at the wild flames is like facing my demons as they dance and laugh before me. I contemplate my options, foreseeing that Matilda shall send word to Edward and it is undeniable that he shall show no mercy. Who knows what cruel activity would come to mind, feed me to the dogs, throw me in the moat? For Edward's wrath hath no bounds.

I may expect no support from William, who has retreated like a timid deer on the hunt. It grieves me that my foes have cast the portcullis between Tenwyn and I, my dearest companion and only ally. My only hope is to yet relieve myself of the burden within my belly, that I may have cause to deny that I ever have been with-child; that indeed it was poor ale that brought forth my ailments.

Three bottles of the potion remain and although the instructions are to take it at sun-up, I have no time left. I shall take it now, for this is the only route attainable.

Feeling around the bottom of the chest, I am unable to trace any of the bottles. In a fit of pique, I toss all my clothes aside to find nothing there, save two small bags of coins. I call out to Mary. 'Why have you been routing in here?' I shout accusingly.

She stands before me trembling like a hunted pigeon. 'Mistress Matilda asked if there were any other bottles and commanded me to seek them out. She took them away my lady. Pray forgive me.' The girl is petrified. She shall be mindful that I struck her predecessor. She has betrayed me, yet a change has come over me, for I have not the heart to *condemn her. She is but a hapless child, drawn into and become entangled within this drama.*

Those bottles were my final gateway. Now all avenues are closed.

Chapter 64

I open the door to find Eva standing there with her tiny dog Alfie in her arms. It would seem that he is a permanent fixture since she is rarely seen without him. 'Hi Grace, do you have a couple of minutes for a quick word?' she asks a little awkwardly.

I invite her in, strolling into the kitchen to put the kettle on whilst she removes her boots. I wonder if Rosa has sent her to check up on what's going on.

'I have an apology to make,' she begins tentatively, picking Alfie up from the floor. 'You see, I overheard Mason speaking to you at the pub about ...'

'Me being pregnant?' I finish for her.

'Err, yes. Well, I assumed James knew about it, so I asked him. He said he didn't, but by then it was all too late. I'm so sorry Grace.'

'Well, you can tell them all that I am not,' I say decisively, feeling thankful that I am wearing a baggy tee-shirt to conceal the visible evidence. 'It was all a misunderstanding because I'd been sick, and Mason got the wrong end of the stick.' I lie, but admitting it would bring about a whole array of undesirable repercussions.

Eva appears relieved. 'Well, that's good. You know how quickly rumours spread and I didn't want you to think I'd been shit-stirring.'

'It's ok, and I've already put James's mind at rest.'

'Good, well how are you keeping then? We haven't seen you for a-while at the pub.'

'No, I feel locked out now that James and Rosa are an item.' Eva picks up her mug of coffee sighing. 'I get where you're coming from. Richard did the same to me. One minute we were engaged, the next he was back with his ex. Men!'

'I know, and I'm so sorry to hear that, you don't deserve it Eva. As for me, I feel I've been betrayed by them both. Rosa was, I thought, my best friend.'

'I know. As much as I love Rosa, she has no scruples when it comes to men. Mind you, with her track record, she'll be off with someone else next week. Men are so easily flattered by her.'

'Putty in her hands,' I muse. 'But James cut me dead, so he's just as bad.'

'Yes, he's been saying that it was never serious between you both. He just used you Grace.'

'I've been such a fool Eva and should have known better anyway, me being a married woman. I guess I got what I deserved.' I begin to well up and Eva comes to me wrapping her arms around my shoulders.

'Hey,' she says, 'I'm not judging you. I know how Lawrence treated you, banning you from seeing your friends. You're only young Grace. Do you really want to be treated like this for the rest of your life?' I feel Alfie snuggle up against my ankle, as though he too is trying to comfort me, which brings a smile to my face.

'I know Eva, there are a lot of things that need to change when he returns. I've become a lot stronger since he's been away, and the absence has helped me to gain a greater perspective on things. I shall definitely be standing my ground from now on.' I speak with true conviction, but shudder at a flashback of Lawrence hitting me, and it dawns on me that he may become yet more abusive if I display more strength. Since giving everything a lot more thought recently, my marriage feels like walking a tight-rope. I have decided to give things one last shot, but unless things change, I shall have to pluck up the courage to leave.

Chapter 65

Kathryn has called on me, having heard of my plight, and I am most glad of a friend. Her mutt snuggles in her lap as she sits across from me, still wearing the colours of mourning since the discovery of her false betrothal.

'I daresay the castle walls are humming with reports of my shame. Great jollity shall be savoured by mine enemies,' I say bitterly.

Kathryn strokes her mutt lightly. 'Alas, demise 'ere courts pleasure here in this castle,' she says solemnly. 'William has drafted himself away like a skittish fox.'

I look upon her, plain with elfin features, and yet she has more heart than anyone I know. 'Pray Kat, why have you not turned upon me like the others for my vile sins?'

She looks me squarely in the eye. 'Beth, what you have done was wrong 'tis true, yet you are not the only lady to stray whilst her husband is away at war. It is lamentable that the evidence lies there within your belly, where others have been more fortuitous.'

'Yet Kat I am unworthy, and God is punishing me for my sins.'

Kathryn leans towards me, smiling kindly. 'Do not consider yourself unworthy Beth. What course do you profess to take?'

I rest my hands against my ever-swelling belly. 'I know not what to do. My potion has been drawn from me. Do you know of any concoction that I may acquire?'

She shakes her head. 'Beth, these things are perilous and may kill you. Mayhap it is God's will that you should keep it.'

I laugh. 'In a better world Kat, but not in this one.'

'Is there no chance you may pass it off as Edward's?'

'Nay trust me I would, but he has been gone far too long. In any case Matilda shall betray me, of that, I am sure. I know not what shall become of me Kat. I am so fearful.'

She leans toward me and her mutt jumps to the floor. 'Your husband may assign you to a priory, surely not such a bad fate.'

I rise from my seat and begin pacing up and down clasping my hands. 'You know not my husband Kathryn, for he delights in cruelty, and would sooner have me as cattle fodder.' Kathryn looks up at me, concern on her face. 'Well then, perhaps you should seek refuge there before he returns?'

I shake my head. 'He would have me dragged from the very walls.'

'But he may not do so against the will of the sisters.'

I laugh sardonically. 'When Edward's wrath is kindled, he knows no bounds.'

Kathryn looks shocked. 'Has he ever laid hands on you?'

I stop pacing, fixing my eyes to the ground. 'Yes,' I say, biting my lip.

'Do you have any family who may defend you?'

'My brother Edgar is my only hope, although we have never been close. He will be fighting in the war, but I shall petition his wife Helen forthwith.'

'And Helen, is she kindly?'

'I have met her but once, yet I believe she is herself with child, so she may share a sisterly care.' As I speak, I know that her backing would be at the behest of her husband. 'There are no other routes open to me. I must but try.'

Kathryn rises from her chair, causing indignation to her mutt. I move towards her, taking her hands in my own. 'How do you fare?' I ask her. She looks down, 'surviving as I must,' she laughs bitterly.

'You are gracious for coming to my side Kat,' I say looking into her eyes. 'Pray inform me should you hear anything.'

'Of course, Beth.' She raises her black skirts and retreats from my chamber with her mutt following at her feet.

I bid Mary to bring forth my writing materials.

Chapter 66

'So, if you found the scan upsetting, are you sure you're doing the right thing?' Mason moves his empty plate to the side of the table, whilst I still pick away at my sandwich.

'I don't have a choice, do I?'

'Grace, we all have choices. It's obvious you're not happy with Lawrence and he doesn't deserve you. Do you really want to be with a man who abuses you? I know it's not easy, but you could leave, make a fresh start somewhere? Do you have any relatives you could go to?'

'Only a brother who lives in Sussex, but we're not close. I haven't seen him for years. Actually, I've given everything a lot of thought and have decided to give it one last crack. Lawrence might be more stable when he gets home, having been away for a long time. Hopefully he won't get back until after the abortion.' I can tell by his face that Mason is not convinced that things will change when Lawrence returns and find myself slipping into a daydream, conjuring up a picture of living in a little country cottage, watching my daughter dance amongst the flowers in the garden. I find myself smiling at my fanciful notions and at the assumption of it being a girl. It is but a pretty picture and will never be more than that.

As I drive to the stables the next day, I realise that Lawrence hasn't contacted me for a couple of days. I've been so caught up in everything that I'd barely noticed it before. It's been a welcome break, but I can't help but wonder why. Perhaps he is really busy at work, or more likely, he is pissed with me for some reason.

Caesar greets me pricking his ears and I set to mucking out his stable and feeding him fresh hay, even though my leg is stiff today. 'We will go riding again one day Caesar, I promise you,' I say offering him a carrot, which he grabs readily. Somehow as he munches, watching me with his wise eyes, I get a strong impulse that he understands and that he seeks to allay my feelings of guilt.

When I arrive home, I find a letter on the coffee table addressed to me formerly, as Mrs Charlton. It is from Margot, informing me that her mother has taken ill again, and she's gone back to France. It is short, concise, and neatly signed. I smile at the prospect of having some freedom again, at least for a little while.

Chapter 67

Mary has a letter for me. I grab it from her eagerly in expectation that Helen has responded to my plea, but on breaking the seal, I see that it bears Tenwyn's signature. He says he has been denied entry into the castle and may only be of service to me now from afar, since he is embarking on a tour to London to find a new appointment that he may continue to support his family. He goes on to say that he shall correspond whenever able and bids me every success in my quandary.

I take the letter to the fire and watch it become consumed by hungry flames. I assume it unlikely that I shall see my dearest friend again and my heart aches at the prospect. I am quite alone.

There is a knock at the door, and I stand in trepidation as Mary goes to open it, that it may be Matilda or Father Arthur, but breathe a deep sigh of relief at the sight of Kathryn. She rushes towards me in a perturbed state and I feel a sudden twitch in my belly. 'Beth,' she says breathlessly, 'your husband has been wounded and is to be despatched home.'

'It is perplexing that I, his wife, have not been informed of such. How did you come to hear?'

'It was your brother who petitioned Matilda.'

'Really? How odd. I wonder if she were considering informing me, his lady wife? Are you aware of the severity of his wounds?' I ask. I have long held sinful thoughts, that he *may be defeated in battle, thus incapable of returning to torment me.*

She shakes her head. 'I know not of his injury, though I understand it is sufficient that he may no more do battle.'

Now my only hope is that he may not make the journey home, perhaps dying from a raging infection, suffice that when he returns, he is too weak to chastise me severely.

My fate lies now in the mercy of God. I cross myself and drop to my knees, praying to our lady Mary, mother of Christ. And I experience a miracle. She has heard my prayers and is comforting me, for I can feel her hands placed upon my shoulders. An overwhelming sense of love comes over me and I smile at her graceful message, that I am not and never shall be alone.

Chapter 68

Elizabeth appears uneasy as she stands waiting for her maid to open the door to her chamber, then relaxes a little when her friend comes in, carrying her dog in her arms as always. It looks as though she's in a hurry, quickly imparting information to Elizabeth, then bolting off. Whatever she said seems to have left Elizabeth in a state of alarm.

I watch as she falls to her knees performing the sign of the cross, instantly morphing into a cameo portrait of a woman virtuous and serene. To an outside observer, merely by the posture, she appears peaceful, but I know it is illusory. Her sadness is palpable, and my heart goes out to her. She seems so lost and devoid of her usual feistiness, as though she has given up on everything.

I mentally kneel down behind her, admiring her long hair arranged expertly into a braid reaching all the way down her back, and I place my hands upon her slender shoulders, praying for her, her child and for my own. It is all I can do for her. After a-while, as though she is able to sense me, Elizabeth brings her right hand up to her left shoulder and rubs it gently. Then she shifts her gaze down to her stomach, placing her hands there outlining a bump, which appears to be a little more advanced than my own, though it is likely accentuated by her slender frame.

Chapter 69

Spending so long in prayer I have lost all sense of time, and as I rise up, my knees are stiff and sore from kneeling. My chamber has become my gaol, for shame and fear of ridicule keeps me from venturing out. Its walls are stifling, closing in on me in every moment as I stand in wait for news from Helen, my only remaining hope. My wits are fraught in the knowledge that Edward is on his way back.

I draw my cloak around my shoulders and climb up the winding stone steps, feeling the air freshening the higher I go. Reaching the top I am quite breathless, my body still weak from the episode with Agnes's potion. The usual lazy guard is there and on seeing me, he silently retreats, which he is now accustomed to doing. The turret has been my only refuge of late. I miss riding and wonder what fate awaits my beloved Pharaoh when Edward returns.

I cherish the views from here, looking to the road that zig zags all the way to the hills. I seek a messenger who may bring news from Helen, but all I can see is a wagon bearing supplies and a serf carrying a stack of wood upon his back, seemingly drawn fresh from the forest.

I feel a twinge in my stomach and place my hands there protectively, then move them away abruptly. What a ridiculous notion that I even presume to be fond of this thing within my belly, when it is the cause of my downfall. What is this change that procures me to become so soft and doltish?

I hear a scuttling on the steps. It is Mary. 'My lady, you have a visitor,' she calls up to me.

I walk back down the steps uneasily, now always in dread of who may be calling on me, yet when I arrive I see it is another visit from Kathryn, appearing ill at ease. 'Beth,' she utters breathlessly, 'Matilda despatched a messenger to Dover for your husband, and there is rumour that Edward may have arrived there already.' I begin to feel unsteady on my feet and Kathryn helps me to my chair. Staring blankly into space I cross myself silently. Kathryn holds my hand. 'Is there nowhere you may go?'

'I am waiting on my sister-in-law. I may have to take a chance and ride there to Sussex in the hope that she shall entertain me.' I shout out to Mary, 'post-haste prepare me some food and my belongings, and I shall need an escort.' I turn to see her shocked face. 'And keep my counsel, not a word to anyone,' I caution.

Kathryn allows her fidgeting mutt to jump to the floor. 'Beth, do not leave now, for it is a long journey and it is perilous travelling in darkness.'

'You are right, I shall leave at sun-up.' I clasp Kathryn's hands. 'Thank you, Kat, for being such a faithful friend.'

Chapter 70

I open my journal to document what I have just witnessed. Elizabeth's friend with the dog visited her, appearing to be a harbinger of bad news yet again. As usual, being a mere observer of a silent movie was insufficient to comprehend what was happening. The only thing I am able to document is that the information imparted by her friend caused Elizabeth to raise her hand to her face and almost lose her balance in apparent shock. Soon after, her friend picked up her dog and left, whilst Elizabeth began nervously flurrying around, getting her maid to pack up her belongings, as if in preparation for a journey. After a-while, Elizabeth dropped to her knees and I stayed with her, both of us praying together.

Once I have written my notes, I start to read my journal back from the very beginning. It is like a jigsaw, putting the pieces into place, slowly illustrating a picture. Unfortunately, there are a number of gaps, which, with no audible accounts, will never get filled without a certain amount of guesswork or intuition. There are by now so many over-lapping events with my own life, that I can't put it down to coincidence anymore. Thanks to Mason, I no longer view the visions as a threat to my mental health, or as an intrusion on my life, but have come to accept them as an integral part of my being. As soon as I stopped from resisting, my affinity with Elizabeth seemed to open up, along with a strong desire to protect her as I would a close friend or sister. That we are one and the same having different experiences, is too complex for me to come to terms with at the moment, so I prefer to look on her as a separate entity. Maybe we are both fulfilling a contract to assist one another through tough times. Obviously, I cannot judge how I may be helping her, but I like to think she knows on some level that she is not alone. For certain, she is a strong courageous woman and I know that some of her fortitude has rubbed off on me.

Chapter 71

My belly has been twitching aplenty, as if the thing inside is as restive as I am. I indulge in a moment of melancholy for it, all too aware of how it feels to be disregarded and unloved. It is a burden to bear of my own making, a punitive reminder of my sin, and yet it is but a hapless victim in all of this.

I look about my chamber. Mary has packed my belongings and sought out an escort, a young page boy of ten years, being the best she was able to do at such short notice. Once I am dressed in my riding habit, I make my way up to the turret one last time to see if a messenger may be on his way with news from Helen. There is a biting chill in the air as large droplets of rain begin to hurl down. Fixing my gaze upon the road, I become aware of a small band of men on horseback coming our way and, to my dismay, the banner heralding them bears my husband's colours; the shield and cross of blue and gold. They appear to be moving at a fast pace.

In a fit of frenzy, I descend the steps like lightning, raising my skirts high to avoid stepping on them. There is no time to stop at my chamber, so I keep hastening down the small winding steps around and around, seeming to go on and on forever. My haste is interrupted by a guard desiring to ascend. He looks bemused, for it is as unmaidenly as it is precarious, for a lady to hasten the steps as I am. He makes way for me and I finally reach the bottom, entering into the great hall. I hope that when Mary becomes aware of my flight, she shall send the page and my baggage after me.

I make haste to the stables. Master Hedyn is in converse with an old man, halting abruptly as I hasten towards him, flushed and breathless. 'My lady?' he enquires.

'Prepare my horse post-haste,' I command. He sends forth instructions to a young stable-hand and I begin pacing impatiently. Then I irk him further by interrupting their conversation again. 'I am in need a crop,' I declare, since my own lies within my chamber.

'There are none to spare my lady.'

'Then fetch me one that I may borrow,' I snap. He looks at me ungraciously, then walks away, returning with a crop a moment later. 'I bow my head in thanks. 'Where is that boy? I must have my horse NOW.' I am quite unable to conceal the hysteria in my voice. Hedyn looks at me quizzically then shouts at the boy to hasten. After what appears to have been a lifetime, Pharaoh is brought to me at the ready. I am helped astride, and make a rush towards the drawbridge, which auspiciously is down, and I cross myself in gratitude. I keep my head bowed low beneath the hood of my cloak as I make my way across, yet all is ill-timed, for my husband's men are ahead advancing towards me. Edward is not there, no doubt he is kept in the wagon behind because of his injuries, but I recognise his commander in chief heading the small band of men, and by ill luck he sees me.

'There she is!' he shouts. Leaving the drawbridge, I kick Pharaoh, steering him to a sharp right and work him into a fast run. 'Hail Mary, full of grace!' I cry as I hear shouts behind me. Mud flies up from the ground and the rain rushes down so hard that I may barely see ahead. My mind is so beclouded with fear that I feel I am within a dream. I can *almost detect my heart beating as I drive Pharaoh on yet faster.*

Now I know how the deer feels on the hunt, paralysed by fear of impending death. The thud of hooves and men's shouts seem to be become ever louder, echoing all around me. I kick Pharaoh and risk a glance over my shoulder to see how they are advancing.

Chapter 72

I've been tossing and turning for most of the night in trepidation of the day ahead, and Elizabeth has been on my mind a lot. I have barely slept but reassure myself that by tomorrow it will all be over, and I'll be able to put the fact that I was pregnant behind me completely and move forward. It's going to be a long day and I'm feeling shabby and my nerves are jangled, so I decide some meditation should help to settle my mind.

Before I know it, the mirror is there in my mind's eye, and a scene unravels straight away revealing Elizabeth standing at the top of a turret in a long dark cloak with its hood covering her head. She appears to be searching for something on the horizon. Then, all of a sudden, she throws a hand up to her face, appearing shocked and panicked, and starts to run quickly down the long winding castle steps, nearly colliding with a soldier on his way up.

When she reaches the bottom, she quickly makes her way to the stables. I assume she is waiting for her horse to be tacked as I watch her pacing up and down anxiously, and by the time her horse is brought to her, she appears to be at her wits end. Once mounted, she makes her way to the drawbridge, guardedly keeping her head down as she crosses. On reaching the other side, she appears to be nervous on seeing a group of men on horseback, one of whom points at her, shouting. I feel my own fear rise as

Elizabeth turns her horse quickly and shoots off, but they are soon on her tail chasing after her.

I feel panicked, my heart beating frantically, hammering in my ears. Adrenalin pumps through my veins like ice and electric shocks shoot through my head. I am the prey on the hunt chased by a pack of rabid dogs, riding for my life against all the elements as wind and rain lash at me, mud flies and the heavy thud of hooves echo all about me. The craggy terrain is hazardous, with menacing rocks hidden beneath the undergrowth, and at times my horse struggles to grip on the boggy ground. There is a slight resistance as I grip him with my thighs and whip him into a gallop, yet he faithfully complies. I call out a plea to Mother Mary, urging my horse on yet faster, then dare to snatch a look behind me to see how they are advancing, but in my state, all appears as just a haze.

I become aware of my horse stumbling, tripping on a rock, and my world switches to slow motion as I feel myself being thrust from my horse, falling to the ground, landing with a heavy thud. My screams seem to echo as though they are from a faraway place.

From a cloud of darkness, my awareness is suddenly jolted back to the bedroom, tears bursting forth like water from a dam, spilling down my face. I feel the muscles of my chin tremble like a small child and look to the window as if the light could soothe me. Having experienced Elizabeth's trauma first-hand, I feel battered and bruised. Squeezing my eyes shut, I see her lying motionless in the long undergrowth next to her horse, blood oozing from her head, which looks like it struck a rock as she went down.

'She is dead,' I weep. 'Her baby as well, on the very day my own is to die.' I sob long and hard, unable to shift the image of her lying there all alone in the mud, mourning her and her child. I have no idea why I was called to share that harrowing experience with Elizabeth, but on some level, I have a knowing that things shall never be quite the same again.

I become aware of the clock, jolting my senses back to reality with a warning that time will not stand still, and that I should get ready to go to the hospital. I sit back down on the bed as my hands are still shaking and find myself staring into space, still in a state of shock that stuns me to silence; a sense of being frozen in time. I become immersed in a deep stillness where I pray for Elizabeth and her child. A strength and defiance is slowly building from within, ushering in new clarity and conviction. 'No!' I shout out, placing my hands over my stomach, speaking to my child for the first time. 'Elizabeth lost her life and her baby, but I vow that no harm shall come to you. No one is going to take you away from me and I promise to do everything I can to protect you.' Then I look up with tears in my eyes, saying, 'I am doing this for us, Elizabeth, for you and for me.'

I still feel strange and shaky as the horse chase felt so real. I suppose in a sense I was re-living it all, but whilst Elizabeth died, her soul lives on in me. The recent challenges in my life made me feel quite powerless, but on reflection, there were always choices and opportunities there that I just didn't see. I don't have to stay in a loveless marriage or continue seeing myself as a victim. Elizabeth has given me the courage and strength I need to take the reins and charge to my own destiny.

I grab my bag packed ready for the hospital and fling it across the room, then standing on a chair, drag down the large suitcase from the top of my wardrobe, hurling it on the bed and frenziedly begin to pack. I have no idea where I shall go, just so long as it is as far away as possible from Lawrence and James. The important thing is that I am leaving with my baby safe within the comfort of my womb. I know this is the right thing to do, for my heart has been telling me so all along. Although I am still shaken, I am completely at peace with the decision I have made.

Leaving the suitcase half packed for now, I quickly shower, dress then rest with a coffee to collect my thoughts before Mason arrives. I could ring him to tell him about my change of heart, but it would be easier to explain it all face to face. I ponder on whether it would be best to leave home before Lawrence returns, or wait to explain everything to him face to face. The latter seems the honourable thing to do, but who knows what his temper would drive him to, and I don't want to take any chances. I flinch as I glimpse another flashback of Elizabeth lying in the mud-soaked grass and wonder why she was chased. Perhaps her husband returned from wherever he had been and got to find out that she was pregnant? The thought sends a shiver down my spine when I consider all the synchronicities we have shared, and I can't help but wonder if witnessing her death was a precursor to my own fate.

I am unable to find the hospital letter to cancel my appointment, certain that I left it right next to the phone. Margot must have tidied it up, and I swear at my carelessness for leaving something so confidential lying around for prying eyes to find. Eventually I have to contact the doctor's surgery to get the number.

Lawrence may come home any day, so I shall have to prepare quickly, then book myself into a bed and breakfast somewhere to consider my next move. I decide that I shall do more packing later, once Mason has been and gone.

I hear movement downstairs. Margot's in France and it can't be Mason as he doesn't have a key. It has to be James, most likely coming back to retrieve his belongings. But he will be disappointed when he discovers that I have thrown away everything that he left behind. I was a fool to entrust him with a key and will make sure I get it back. He has a nerve coming here and letting himself in like this!

I creep downstairs to the hallway noticing the front door has been left wide open and a big black suitcase is perched by the door. Then it dawns on me, it is not James. Lawrence is home! I jolt when I see him, still in his black wool coat, as he storms from the kitchen then becomes aware of me hovering on the stairs. I notice his hair is shorter than usual in a military cut, shaved shorter at the sides, and his tanned face is flushed red with anger. 'There you are!' he shouts, and I start at his threatening manner.

'Lawrence, what are you doing here, back so soon?' I utter, nervously backing away as he strides towards me at the foot of the stairs.

'You little bitch!' he barks, boiling with rage. The last time I saw that look on his face was when he hit me.

'What?' I cry as he slaps me hard across the face, sharply stinging my cheek.

'Been enjoying yourself have you while I've been slaving my bollocks off? While the cat's away, eh?'

I have no idea how much he knows or how he could have found out anything. I start walking towards the kitchen to get away from him, but he is fast on my tail. 'Lawrence please don't do this,' I whimper. 'You've just got back. At least let me get you a drink, then we can talk. I don't know what you've heard, but I'm sure I can explain everything.'

'Oh yes my dear, you have a lot of explaining to do. Margot has told me everything, you little tart. I know all about your boyfriend and how he's knocked you up. How dare you!' He comes at me and I sidestep to avoid him pinning me against the wall, then run through the kitchen and out the back into the garden. He comes after me, pulling me back by my long hair and I shriek out in pain, stumbling against a kitchen chair. Now he comes at me, threatening with his fist. 'You little slut.'

I step backwards, shielding my stomach with one hand and my face with the other. 'Lawrence please, can't we just talk?' I plea.

'Talk? Don't you think you've left it a bit late for that? I always knew you were a whore, that you'd betray me.' I brace myself as he throws me against the wall and spits in my face. I cower to the floor terrified, waiting for the next blow. But then I become aware of someone creeping up behind him. On hearing a noise, Lawrence turns his head and then Mason hurls a cricket bat at him, delivering a blow at full force to his head, sending him reeling to his feet, groaning, and clutching hold of his bleeding head. I am trembling like a storm-struck tree as Mason helps me up from the floor, then quickly calls the emergency services on his phone. I look over at Lawrence groaning and cursing, too weak to move, blood forming a pool on the floor next to him from the gash on his head.

'Oh my God,' I cry, unable to stop from trembling.

'Are you okay?' Mason asks, brushing my hair away from my face and bringing his arm around my shoulder.

'I will be when that bastard is out of my life. You couldn't have timed it better. Where did you get the cricket bat from?'

'I always keep it in my car, just as well, eh? I heard you shouting when I arrived to come to pick you up.' I see Mason is also in shock, hardly surprising as he is not one predisposed to violence.

I gasp as Lawrence tries to get to his feet, but Mason is quick to react, standing over him, the bat raised in the air as a warning.

'No you don't mate, you're staying right there until the police arrive,' he says. I fetch a tea towel from the drawer and toss it down on the floor next to Lawrence and he holds it over his head to stem the bleeding. He looks up. 'So you're the bastard boyfriend I take it, who has been fucking my wife?' he says. His words are slurred, and I wonder if it is because of the blow to his head, or, more likely, that he arrived here in a drunken state.

'No,' I reply coldly. 'Mason is a friend of mine.'

Mason turns to me. 'You need to go and sit down. I'll keep an eye.' Lawrence suddenly grabs his leg as we are both caught off-guard, bringing him down, and they get into a scuffle thrashing about on the floor. Mason shouts to me, 'get out, take my car!'

'No, I can't leave you,' I say, trying to think quickly what to do. Mason manages to writhe free from his grip and clambers to his feet rushing towards me, and we make a mad dash to his car in the driveway. I get there first, automatically jumping into the driver's seat. The keys are in the ignition, but in my panic I stall the car. 'Move over, I'll drive,' Mason says pushing me to the passenger's side and starting the engine. I look back over my shoulder to see Lawrence, still holding the blood-soaked tea towel on his head, making his way to his BMW.

'Quick Mason!' I shout out and we career down the road. Mason tosses his mobile at me instructing me to call the police. The operator asks too many questions and I find myself interrupting her. 'Look, my friend Mason Tenner has called you already about my violent husband. We are no longer in my house, but now he is chasing us in our car. We are in a blue Mondeo and Lawrence Charlton is in a black BMW. We are travelling south on the Kempton Road, heading towards Chiggingworth. Please hurry, my husband is deranged, and I think he might be drunk.' I surprise myself with my composure, even as my hands are still trembling.

As I hang up, I look back over my shoulder and see Lawrence is beginning to catch us up, his headlights blinding. With only cat's eyes for lighting, visibility ahead is abysmal on this quiet country road, especially as rain is lashing hard against the windscreen. Mason pushes the peddle to gain more distance from Lawrence and I clutch onto the sides of my seat as we take a bend too quickly, closing my eyes in terror. And then I see Elizabeth on her horse in a blind panic retreating from a group of angry men. I gasp out loud at the realisation. All seems to have brought me to this moment; the synchronicities, visions and insights, all melding into one. I witnessed Elizabeth's fate ... and so, now I know what mine will be.

I look back to see Lawrence right on our tail. 'What now?' I ask timidly.

'I guess he will try to ram me when he gets the chance, but he can't do anything on this narrow road, not until there's a passing area.' He accelerates harder and I close my eyes and pray.

'I hear a siren. The police are coming!' I shout, looking back over my shoulder, seeing blue flashing lights advancing on Lawrence. As I turn back, I notice lights coming at us as we take a bend too fast. 'Slow down!' I shout as Mason jams on his brakes, then Lawrence smashes into the back of us, jolting us both forward, but thankfully we both had the foresight to put on our seatbelts.

I slump back in my seat catching my breath, overwhelmed by the sound of sirens and blue flashing lights lighting up the darkness and illuminating the deluge of rain. The car ahead that we nearly collided with turns out to be another police car and has been expertly manoeuvred sideways onto the road. Mason swears under his breath whilst undoing his seatbelt, then turns to me. 'Are you ok love?' he asks softly.

'I am now,' I grin, even though I feel sick and my hands are shaking violently.

The remainder of the night is a haze of countless questions and statements at the police station, then finally, I find myself here in a hospital bed exhausted, yet grateful to be alive. I guess it was my destiny to be in a hospital today, but not for a termination. My baby is still with me, by all accounts unscathed. My connection with Elizabeth was severed on this fateful day as our paths divided. Unlike her, my child and I both survived the chase.

Mason is at my bedside, holding my hand tenderly. I have told him all about my vision this morning that resulted in a change of heart about the termination. 'She helped me Mason, for when I witnessed her demise, I realised I had to venture away from the destructive path that I was on, and my heart had been telling me all along to keep the baby. I have Elizabeth to thank and you too Mason for saving us,' I say, placing his hand on my swollen belly, feeling a twitch as

I do so. 'Did you feel that?' I ask, but it was evidently too faint, as he shakes his head grinning.

'It's an incredible story Grace and I'm sure you helped Elizabeth too on some level.'

'I hope so, though I don't think I will ever truly understand what it was all about.'

'We don't need to understand everything love. Life is a succession of experiences, both good and bad. Think how tedious it would be if there was no magic or mystery.'

That night, as I close my eyes, I see Elizabeth's face smiling at me. She looks jubilant, with a serenity about her I have never before witnessed and a strong sense that she is at peace. After a few seconds the vision fades, but I know that she is always there because she is a part of me.

Epilogue

Hello Grace, on behalf of the *Woman's Herald*, congratulations on the success of your best-selling book, For *Elizabeth*. It's a very interesting story and you described how a horse-riding accident seemed to spark up dreams and visions of another lifetime, that you believe was your own. Can you in any way describe how these visions presented themselves?

Well, I observed them through my inner eye. The only way I can describe it to you is that they were more vivid than dreams and more life-like than movies, but not exactly 3D. As I only had visuals, I had to try to piece everything together, with a certain amount of guesswork. Even though I saw Elizabeth as the third person, somehow, I could identify with her, even experiencing her emotions. It could be quite exhausting at times.

Why did you call the book For *Elizabeth*?

It was a dedication to a courageous lady. I had to call her something, so chose Elizabeth after my middle name.

Do you think she influenced you in any way?

Yes, definitely. I'm sure I acquired some of her feistiness, which I needed at a very testing time in my life. I was on a destructive path and she became the bridge to a much brighter one. God only knows where I could have ended up otherwise and I have a beautiful daughter, Elizabeth, in her namesake.

Do you think you influenced Elizabeth?

On the level you're talking about it's impossible for me to know, but I'm sure she was able to sense my presence at times, so I like to think so. On a spiritual level, undoubtedly, because we share the same soul, something I tend to forget because it's so hard to comprehend.

Do you still have visions?

No, everything stopped on the day she died.

What happened to your horse?

Ah, thank goodness I am able to ride Caesar again. Curiously, my courage returned after Elizabeth's fateful ride, though I'm a little less reckless than I used to be.

What about Lawrence, are you still in contact with him?

No, we have nothing to say to each other. The divorce should be finalised soon. I wish him no malice, but it's good to be free from his shackles. Actually, I am grateful to him, for he taught me such a lot. As the saying goes, adversaries are our greatest teachers.

Do you still see Mason?

Very much so. We live together and have our own baby boy, William. Mason is my soul-mate and he is the best father. He came into my life at the right time and saved me on so many levels. I adore him.

How is Elizabeth with her baby brother?

She completely dotes on him, although she is quite bossy.

So what do you think you have learned from your experiences?

Where do I start? I am a lot stronger now and it's obviously changed my whole outlook on life. I no longer see myself merely as Grace Charlton, for I've come to believe we are all multi-dimensional beings. I've done a lot of reflecting on how times have changed, particularly for women. Today we have more freedom to make our choices, whereas Elizabeth, even as a woman of privilege, seemed to have both her hands bound.

What do you say to people who disbelieve your story?

I can only speak for myself, that my experiences were very real to me. I could so easily have slipped through the net in the belief that I was mentally ill. In different times, and without Mason's support, my path could have taken me down a spiral of medication and psychiatrists, whereas my life has actually been enriched on so many levels.

Do you think things are changing at all, that there is more acceptance of these matters?

Paranormal phenomena continues to fall into the category of 'nonsense' because it can't be scientifically proven, though

yes, I believe awareness is growing and people are slowly opening up to new concepts.
Final word?

I would just like to reiterate a cliché we have all heard before; that however bad things appear to be, I believe there is purpose in everything that happens to us. We are both teachers and students playing out unique and individual roles, creating drama in collaboration with one another as villains and victims. I believe we are far more powerful than we realise, and we should all acknowledge the magic and miracles in the stories that we call our lives.

"All the world's a stage.

And all the men and women merely players:

They have their exits and their entrances;

And one man in his time plays many parts,

his acts being seven ages."

As you like it
William Shakespeare

Author's note

Jane has two children and two grandchildren. Born in England, she now lives in Turkey with her husband, Ian. Living close to the sea with a mountainous backdrop provides the perfect setting for her writing.

Other books by Jane are:

Journey to Forever, 2017
Mirror of Grace, 2019
Dark Star, 2021
Power of the Shadow, 2022

"Grace carried me here and by grace I will carry on."

Printed in Great Britain
by Amazon